Games of Ruin

KJ Rivers

Published by KJ Rivers, 2024.

This is a work of fiction. Similarities to real people, places, or events are entirely coincidental.

GAMES OF RUIN

First edition. January 31, 2024.

Copyright © 2024 KJ Rivers.

ISBN: 979-8989863105

Written by KJ Rivers.

This book is for us, the broken ones. The ones who can't close their eyes without wanting to cry. For those who have to fight so hard to just be okay. For the unlucky and the unheard. I see you, I am you.

"The only family I have left are the bittersweet memories of a traumatic past and the only loyal friend I can call my own is the brokenness inside of me. I am sentenced to life on earth and all I want is to truly live yet I am stuck simply surviving, my hope of a future has been dimmed by an unrelenting past, promising to give me a life of misery. So I am doing the best that I can, I am not living, I am surviving at best."

- K.J. Rivers

Preface

This book contains depictions of mental health disorders, violent rivalry, and captivity. It takes place in a prison-like setting that is a fictional place and is in no way based on a real-life place or institution.

The characters in this story often joke about their mental illnesses and trauma. This book contains dark content. It merely depicts my personal experience with mental health disorders and expresses what it's like from my perspective. I understand everyone's experience is different. I am in no way trying to reduce the seriousness of these disorders. Please don't read this book if you are sensitive to these dark themes.

If you are struggling with mental health issues and are thinking of hurting yourself in some way, please talk to somebody and get help. This world needs you. You are important. You matter.

National hotline 1-800-273-8255

Acknowledgement

The first person I want to say thank you to is my best friend. He is someone who has never let me down, someone I have leaned on time and time again. This person's love is unconditional and I wouldn't be here without him. In fact, nobody would be. His name is Jesus, the Lord of Lords and King of Kings. You are my everything and I'll never be able to thank you enough.

Next, I'd like to thank my Husband, the man who believed in me when I couldn't believe in myself. You continue to amaze me every day, the day I met you I found the missing half of myself. You make me want to be a better person, a person deserving of a love like yours. Thank you for encouraging me to write this book and for showing up for me every step of the way. My heart beats for you and you alone, I will always love you.

Next, I want to thank the K and the J who make up my name. You know who you are. Truth be told, I wouldn't be alive if it weren't for these two incredible human beings. You saved my life more than once and never asked for anything in return. You've never not been at my side. Your loyalty knows no bounds and I'm so grateful to have you guys in my life. Our bond is everlasting and I'll spend my lifetime trying to repay you for everything you've done for me. Truth be told, all words fall short regarding how important you are to me but just know I love you guys.

Lastly, I want to say thank you to my readers. This dream of mine wouldn't be possible without your support. I hope you enjoy the book and I wish each and every one of you a lifetime of happiness.

Content Warning

This story contains content that may be troubling to some readers including but not limited to violence, death, abduction, drug use, mild profanity, and conversations of sexual assault and rape. This book also contains depictions of mental illness including but not limited to depression, anxiety, trauma, PTSD, abuse, and self-harm. Please be mindful of these and possible other triggers and seek assistance if needed.

Prologue

<u>*The Sibling Of David Williams*</u>
I've been through extraordinary pain, pain you couldn't even begin to fathom. My backstory is sad enough, the pieces are perfectly placed for me to become a villain, but that's just not who I am. I was brought up by an abusive father and an absent mother, both of whom had no business being parents. I'll spare you the gory details, all you really need to know is that it's always just been me and my older brother, David against the world. It was a miracle we even made it out of the situation alive.

David could have run, it would have been easier for him to leave me behind. But instead, he did the harder thing, the honorable thing, and took me with him. He dropped out of school and worked three jobs to make sure I was taken care of. He was a better parent than my Mother and Father combined, and I shouldn't have even been his responsibility. But he didn't see it that way, to him, I wasn't a burden. He was all I had, and it was enough.

As soon as I was old enough, I secured my first job. My brother never let me drop out of school, but I insisted on helping financially. So anytime I wasn't at school, I was working at my minimum-wage job, just trying to help my brother get by. I was hardly ever home, even still my brother and I were inseparable, I owed him my life.

Then, in the blink of an eye, David was dead. His death shattered me entirely, the world lost its color, and I was left numb. Nothing mattered anymore, I was hollow and broken, the only person I had ever loved was gone, and I didn't know how I was supposed to continue living this cruel life. Everything changed that day.

As time went on, I grew to despise the thing that killed him. Each year yielded more and more hatred. I got to the point where I couldn't even remember a time when I wasn't consumed by resentment. I had a choice to make, I could either let the pain destroy me, or I could use it to fuel something extraordinary. I chose the latter and promised myself I'd rid the world of the thing that killed my brother and that I'd actually make a difference, in his name. That's why I started all of this.

I'm going to tell you what I did but first, I just want to start by saying that I know my choices are morally wrong. Ethically, I am a villain, I break all the rules of a governed society. I am not without flaws, I make mistakes like everyone else. I'm not naive enough to believe that people will see me as the hero of this story. Do I think they should? Of course, I do. But ultimately it's all about perspective. The best heroes are willing to sacrifice the few to save the many and that's exactly what I'm doing.

A few examples of this include Robin Hood and Christopher Columbus. Robin hood stole from the rich, but then he gave that money to the poor. He did something morally wrong, but because it was for a good cause, he is considered a hero. Christopher Columbus killed and enslaved the natives, and he brought them new diseases among other things. But because he intended to spark the Atlantic exploration, trade, and European colonization, he is worshiped in schools.

These examples show that doing the unethical thing for a good cause, still makes you a hero. Keep that in mind as I tell you what I did.

After my brother died, I met a man named James. When I first saw him, every cell in my body told me he was evil, and over time, I grew to understand that he had no regard for human life. He wasn't the partner in crime I wanted, I was hoping for someone with a little more of a soul, but I didn't have a lot of options, and he had money, a lot of it. So, I brought him an offer he couldn't refuse, I'd be the brains, and he'd get to kill.

We started immediately and when a factory in the middle of nowhere was listed for sale, it felt like fate. We spent months fabricating every aspect of the place to meet our needs and more importantly, we made it inescapable. I gave James free rein to create what we call "levels" because, after all, he was the psychopath. These levels would test the subjects' strength, mental capacity, and will to survive. Several people would die within these walls, but their sacrifice would not be in vain.

I took on the role of finding staff and test subjects, which proved more difficult than I had anticipated. But eventually, everything came together, I found doctors, janitors, security guards, and scientists. All of whom either believed in our cause or were willing to turn a blind eye for the right price. Everything would have to be perfect for this to work, so I spent countless days ensuring every little detail was right.

KJ RIVERS

I sent out a brochure, offering 2,000 dollars for anyone willing to participate in a clinical trial. The brochure yielded more applicants than I ever thought possible, and I had to sort through them, I couldn't take everyone. I carefully chose the test subjects, these people had no idea that they would change the world with their sacrifice. I picked individuals with good lives and those with bad, I chose rich and poor, smart and dumb, diversity was key. Then I organized the chosen into groups of 15, I fell in love with each and every one of them.

One group I couldn't help but become especially fond of, they had come from broken homes just like me. I wanted so badly to tell them that they would not be suffering in vain but of course, I couldn't, it would compromise the entire study. Amanda was my favorite, I watched her for weeks. She had characteristics that reminded me of David.

It was obvious in the way she held herself that she didn't know how special she truly was. She was strong and brave, and she always stood up for what she believed in. She was feisty and a little too stubborn for her own good, but it always kept me on my toes. Amanda was the gorgeous girl that didn't even know she was beautiful, it wasn't humble, it was just sad. But I would change that, by the end of the study, she would know her true strength if she even made it that far.

Something drew me to Amanda, and I couldn't quite figure out what it was. All I did know was that I would stop at nothing to ensure that there was a place in the study with her name on it. I was excited to watch her become her strongest self, to grow into the person I knew she could be.

But enough about Amanda, the point is that I'm extremely grateful for all of my subjects, and it's going to hurt to watch them suffer. That is why I left James in charge of inflicting pain and killing those who need to die. I'm not a monster, I would never want to kill, I need you to believe that. But I am willing to do whatever needs to be done to extinguish the thing responsible for my brother's death. I will get justice for David, no matter the cost.

Moments like this require someone like me, someone who has the strength to do what no one else dares to do. Someone who will sacrifice the few to save the many, someone who will act. Someone who will do the uncomfortable thing, the crucial thing. And deep down I know that while I actually try to do something with my life, people will judge me and probably call me evil.

But the truth is, this world is cruel, and it needs to change. So is it so wrong that I want to make a difference? Is it so wrong that I'm willing to bend the rules to create something life-changing? Christopher Columbus and Robin Hood did the uncomfortable thing, some would argue the wrong thing but this world still considers them heroes. I'm not asking you to call me a hero, I'm just asking you to not dismiss me as a villain. Just keep an open mind and try to understand.

I don't want to do this, if there was any other way I'd take it. But this is just how it has to be so without further ado, let the study begin.

Chapter One

A<u>manda West</u>

"Starting now," were the only two words transmitted through the intercom. My body flinched at the sound and I began to run, willing my legs to go faster, leaning forward, begging my lungs to gather more air. In this place, I was no longer Amanda, instead, I became a mere number - specifically, number three. This place did not allow for personal identity or individuality.

Here, your existence was merely a test to see how far your body could truly push its limits. I was unsure of how much further I could bend without breaking, but today was not the day for intrusive thoughts, so I shoved them to the back of my mind, praying they'd stay there.

I took a sudden left turn, running towards the sound of rushing water, hoping that the noise would mask my footsteps and ragged breathing. I ran further and further, the water so close now, that I couldn't hear anything else. I stopped at the nearest tree and took the chance to look back at the clearing, assessing my competition. Two bodies lay motionless, their dark red blood slowly seeping into the ground. I gagged and turned away, not letting myself throw up and leave evidence of where I had been.

I forced my eyes back to the clearing, needing to know what direction the psycho was headed. I think his name was James but that hardly mattered right now. I scanned the area, but not a person in sight, or a living one at least. Not seeing him sent a shiver down my spine, despite the 90-degree weather.

Out of the corner of my eye, I saw movement and flinched even though I was yards away. It was number five, I recognized her by her flaming red hair. What was she doing? I wanted to shout to her, tell her to run, but I knew that it was suicide. So I did the only thing I could do, I watched and prayed that she would get away.

James appeared before I could even finish my prayer, locking eyes with number five. Dread filled my insides as James approached. Number five was imprisoned in the same spot, the shock keeping her feet captive. My eyes urged her to take action, whether it be running, hiding, or fighting. I just wanted her to do something.

After an unending infinity, she finally began to run. Her survival instincts took over, overpowering the shock and igniting her adrenaline, all driven by her will to survive. But it was too late. I watched as he grabbed her, tackling her to the ground. A tear slid down my face as she screamed, the sound oozed with desperation.

As much as I wanted to look anywhere else, I could not tear my eyes from the scene. James had her pinned to the ground, a horrific smile on his face and he plunged his knife into her back, once, twice, thrice. The smile grew wider with each thrust.

He scanned the area, searching for his next target. I quickly ducked, willing myself to disappear into the ground beneath me. It wasn't enough, panic filled my veins as I watched James head left into the trees, straight toward me. Instinct took over as I jumped up and began to run. Sadness, anger, and fear threatened to pierce through me, cutting deeper than a knife ever could.

Regardless, I suppressed the emotions, not allowing myself any time to process the horror I had just witnessed or erase his disturbing smile from my mind. In this place, letting emotions surface could be fatal.

I kept my eyes peeled while sprinting as fast as I could. James was not the only predator in these woods and I'd be a fool to let my guard down. I slowed to a steady run, trying to conserve my energy, my body grateful for the change. I needed a plan, where was I even running to? I had no idea where I was.

The stream was the only thing preventing me from getting lost and going around in circles. Even so, it would become a popular place and as much as I hated it, I'd have to leave it behind.

I looked around at my surroundings. Everything looked the same, if I went farther into the woods, I'd be lost but I couldn't stay here. *Think Amanda. Time is running out. Make a decision or you will die.* I wanted to scream, to silence my brain, but panic was engulfing every cell in my body, making it increasingly difficult to compartmentalize.

Just as I began to lose hope, I looked up at the setting sun and threw myself forward, it would be my new guide.

I ran deep into the woods, my heart threatening to burst from my chest. Even deeper, my lungs are crying out, urging me to stop. So deep now, the light is becoming dim, making it hard to see. My guide is nowhere to be seen, overshadowed by the trees. I stopped beside a tree to let my eyes adjust and take the break that my body had been begging for.

Every sound posed a threat, there was danger lurking in every direction waiting to take me by surprise. Staying still was so much worse, my paranoia had succeeded at consuming me entirely, he could be anywhere by now. Surely he would know this place like the back of his hand, right? Which meant he could be close, or even watching me right now.

Goosebumps prickled at my skin, I shook my head, shaking away the thoughts along with it. I needed to keep moving, which way did I come from?

I frantically looked around and noticed that all the trees looked identical. I blinked rapidly. If I went the wrong way, I might run straight into that monster. I needed to climb a tree and locate the sun, otherwise, I would be lost.

I looked around and noticed a tree with low branches. Saying a silent prayer, I began to climb the tree. I got to the second branch before I heard a rustling noise. Footsteps boomed through the woods, coming straight towards me.

My body physically shrank in the tree, trying to hide in the bark. I was vulnerable and with nowhere to run, I was easy prey. The footsteps stopped just below me and I finally dared to look down, my breath trapped in my lungs and my body forgot how to exhale.

Chapter Two

When I looked down, I immediately made eye contact with a man. His intense gaze seemed to penetrate my very soul. The fear in his eyes was a direct reflection of my own, and at that moment, I realized that he was prey, just like me.

Every instinct in my body urged me to climb higher because I knew that fear has the power to turn even the best people into monsters. I wasn't naive enough to think I was safe. I began climbing the tree higher, getting as much distance between us as possible. What else could I do?

He sensed my fear and whispered to me "I don't understand what's going on, I just need help. I'm not going to hurt you," he paused and the silence was oppressive. "I didn't sign up to play this sick game, I want out," he ran a hand through his hair.

I stopped climbing and relief swarmed my body when I realized he wasn't chasing me up the tree.

"You think this is a game? You think we signed up for this? People are dead. I don't know who you are, but this isn't funny and it sure as hell isn't a game," all of my words dripped venom.

"Okay, okay I get it. But one minute I was inside a building and the next I woke up here with people telling me rules, and now I'm freaking being hunted! So excuse me for having questions and excuse me for asking for help." He whispered back, louder this time, and began to walk away in frustration.

"What's your number?" I asked In a whisper. The question caught him off guard, I could tell by the way his eyebrows pulled together.

"15," he replied, and my heart sank. It was the worst number to be assigned, there was no time to adjust or prepare. I couldn't not help him, could I?

"Okay we don't have much time, so I'll explain the basics, but then you have to leave. Deal?" I whispered against my better judgment.

"I swear," he responded, pleading with his eyes.

"There are fifteen of us. Tonight, we are being hunted. The hunt will stop when eight of us are dead. James is the only one with a weapon, but the other numbers will try to kill you to save themselves, so he's not the only threat. That's all you need to know. Trust no one." I began climbing again, I had been in this spot far too long.

"Is he... James hunting us for fun? Are they going to let us go if we survive? I thought one of the rules was we can't kill each other." He raised his voice to accommodate the distance.

Paying no attention to his first question, I responded "I'm not sure if they'll let us go but that doesn't matter right now, right now we just need to focus on making it through the night. We can't kill each other, but some people will do anything to save themselves they'll break your legs, so you can't run from James or make you scream to draw him close. We had a deal, it's time for you to go."

GAMES OF RUIN

It felt unforgivable to make him go, and even though I despised the decision, I could not gamble with my life by placing it in the hands of a stranger.

"I'm going, thanks for your help, I'll see you again when this is all over," he sounded hopeful and I found myself wishing that I could have just an ounce of his confidence. By the time I looked down again, he was nowhere to be seen.

I knew deep down that it was unlikely I'd ever see him again, but I said a prayer for his safety and purged him from my consciousness, I needed to focus.

I scrambled up the last few branches and caught a glimpse of the setting sun. I felt a sense of relief in my core as if the sun's rays could be my salvation right now. I climbed down the tree and began walking in the right direction once again, towards my guide.

Running was no longer a viable choice, it would leave me clueless as to James's whereabouts. So instead, I proceeded carefully, listening out for any potential danger. I closed my eyes for a moment, willing my hearing to advance.

Every chirp made me flinch and every whisper of wind sent a shiver down my spine. At that moment, I heard a scream, full of misery and suffering. It was long and drawn out, belonging to a man.

In my gut, I hoped it wasn't Fifteen. I had only spoken to him once, if he was dead I only had myself to blame. I should have done more and helped him, but I was afraid, and I was a coward. The shriek emanating from my left made me want to take off to the right and get away as quickly as possible, though I knew that wouldn't be wise.

Everyone would be heading that way so instead, I continued straight, praying that it was the right decision. The scream was close, way too close which either meant that James was near, or another threat had arisen.

It is my understanding that individuals always succumb to fear, doing whatever it takes to make it out alive. They will sacrifice you to save themselves, and turn on each other as the threat of death looms over them. But is death the greatest loss in life?

Can a person still be considered a human being after all traces of humanity have been lost? All I know is that three people are dead, maybe more, and every time I close my eyes I see their bodies, lying there, limp. And every time, the guilt consumes me.

As I skirted the tree, I was brought to an abrupt stop. Right in front of me was number 13 greeting me with a piercing stare. I recognized him from my time in captivity and my intuition had told me he was someone that couldn't be trusted.

"How's it going beautiful?" He smirked, amusement dancing in his eyes. His shirt was soaked with blood. I immediately knew I was in danger and began sprinting, with no direction in mind.

I heard him chasing me through the woods, my heart heavy in my ears. My adrenaline forced me to run faster than I ever had before, but it wasn't enough.

I fell to the ground with such force that the entire forest trembled. Thirteen was on top of me, daring me to fight, with no fear in his eyes. I clawed and kicked and adrenaline took over as I was trying to wriggle myself free. He punched me in the face, the metallic taste of blood forming in my mouth.

GAMES OF RUIN

I spat and continued to kick as his fist threatened to attack once again. I gave one last kick, summoning all the force my body would give, and his body broke away. Without hesitation, I jumped up and began to run, my mind dizzy, and my pulse still racing. I had the time to take a few steps before I was back on the ground, this time thirteen had a more powerful grasp, prohibiting my mobility, his claws embedding in my skin.

I braced for whatever he was going to do to me, he couldn't kill me, so maybe I would still have a chance. Maybe I could break free. Still, the terror overwhelmed me, he could make me wish I was dead and that scared me even more than death itself.

He had me in a situation where I couldn't defend myself, and he grinned with satisfaction.

"Let me go freak!" I whispered not wanting James to hear.

"Now why would I do that when we're having so much fun?" When I didn't respond, he continued. "I'm going to set you up to die, but first", he paused, "first, how do you feel about making this day even more exciting?" He asked but it was evident that he had already made up his mind. There wasn't even an ounce of doubt in his voice. I had to get out of here I jerked and wiggled even though it was pointless.

"Don't you know the more you fight, the more I'm going to enjoy it?" He spoke quietly in my ear, his breath scalding my skin as horror began to claw up my throat. I needed to get away, there's always a way I just needed to think. *Think Amanda, think!* I urged myself to find an answer.

My eyes brimmed with tears, and a feeling of helplessness wrapped itself around my heart. I willed my tears not to fall, I would not give him the satisfaction of seeing me cry.

Somehow in my panicked state, I didn't hear the leaves crunching beside me but In an instant, the weight was lifted off of me, and I could breathe again. After that, another thump was perceptible, its vibration echoing in my ears while confusion gnawed at my brain.

Chapter Three

I mustered the strength to stand up, and as my vision cleared, I noticed that Fifteen was towering over Thirteen, holding a rock in his hand. He viciously slammed the rock against Thirteen's temple and stepped away as Thirteen became still.

"D-Did you k-kill him?" I stammered as my mouth hung open in astonishment. My eyes began to widen and my body trembled with fear.

"Please, please, please don't be dead," Fifteen muttered with desperation as he reached down to check his pulse. "He's alive, thank God he's alive," he let out a small sigh.

"If you had killed him..." My mind was still processing what just happened.

"I know, trust me, I know but he would have hurt you, I had to stop him." Fifteen looked me in the eye for the first time.

"How did you find me, and why would you help? You'd have been better off letting me die," I stood up straighter as the shock subsided.

"Trust me, no one would be better off with you dead and you helped me, so I figured I owed you one." He let out a humorless laugh. "Now let's get the hell out of here before we're the next victims."

He walked away, and I had to jog to catch up. Even after he rescued me, a feeling of apprehension echoed in my stomach.

Had he been following me? Anger arose replacing the gratitude and I couldn't help but feel uncomfortable standing by his side.

"Were you following me?" the words flew out before I had time to stop them and I had no time to disguise my glare.

His demeanor changed, and instantly I knew he had been before he so much as uttered a word

"I'm in a place I don't recognize, surrounded by people I don't know. Everyone is out to hurt me so is it so bad that I wanted to stick by the one person who seems to have a soul?" He paused for effect. "I'm sorry, In any other situation, I would have left you alone, and I'm not trying to freak you out, but this is life or death and I just thought safety in numbers and all that." He sounded sincere but trusting someone right now was not a choice, even if he had helped me. Everyone had an agenda and I had no plan to stick around and find out what his was.

"Thanks for the help, but I don't know you or trust you. I'm going right, you go left, don't follow me." I sounded rude, cold even, and I hated it but being nice was a privilege for those who were safe, and I certainly was not.

I ran to the right before he had a chance to protest, but I couldn't help thinking of Thirteen. We had left him there to die. For all I knew, he could be dead already. He was an awful human being but did anyone deserve to die like this?

It was a situation of kill or be killed, but that didn't make it right. I felt the guilt holding me back, making it difficult to run. My thoughts ran circles in my mind, despite my attempts to quiet them.

How much longer would this hunt go on? It was getting dark as if we needed yet another disadvantage. The sun seemed to dissipate too quickly; I guess time flies when you're being hunted for sport.

I started to question how long I had been running when a sharp sound caught my attention.

A scream pierced through the darkness as another victim, a woman pleaded for her life.

I had no time to process or say a prayer for the girl, I needed to run, the scream was close. James was close and I needed to get out of here now. A couple more minutes and I would have run straight into him, I would have been his next victim.

Terror soaked me to the bone as I spun around and bolted with all my strength. Sticks crashed below me, bushes jabbed me with thorns and nothing could stop me now, but I needed stealth on my side.

I was making too much noise, the eerie silence as I slowed pierced my ears like the scream I had heard moments ago. I turned right and walked slowly, with my thoughts echoing loudly in my mind.

I walked cautiously, evading any sticks and leaves, relying on the diminishing light to find my way. I looked to my left, then to my right and I forced my mouth to shut, to stifle the scream caught in my throat.

Three bodies were stacked to my right, with blood scattered everywhere. The pungent, metallic smell of blood filled my nose. How did I not hear their screams? The rushing water must have blocked the sound.

I allowed a few tears to escape before quickly leaving the scene. These were people, they were brothers, sisters, friends, how many people had noticed they were gone? How many people were out there looking for them? I couldn't think like that, not here and not now.

If my calculations were right, one more person would have to die and unless I wanted it to be me, I'd have to fight like hell to survive, I'd have to be strong.

I walked forward, forcing my legs to comply, begging my mind to hold on for a while longer. My body was paralyzed, and each fatality brought more weight to my mental state. My soul teetered on the brink of collapse, but I continued forward. I urge my legs once again to take step after step.

Chapter Four

I heard rustling behind me and froze in my tracts, pausing to breathe, willing my hearing to advance. It was dangerously close, far too close, coming from the spot I had just been. I looked behind me, but darkness had consumed the trees, the dim light completely gone now. My hearing was the only thing I had, and my heartbeat was thudding in my ears, blocking even that.

I wanted to move, to run, but I couldn't give away my position. I heard a thud and sticks cracking and at this moment, I knew that I wasn't going to survive the night. The wrestling became louder, and I heard a voice I didn't recognize "Come out, come out wherever you are" he sang. My heart stopped beating, it was James, I was sure of it. I was about to become his next victim.

I was frozen in place, just like number five had been, but I refused to go down without a fight. I let out a slow quiet breath and bent down. I scavenged the forest floor, wishing for just an ounce of light until I found two rocks. I stood up once again, a rock in each hand.

He was so close now, I could hear his ragged breathing. I took a step forward and threw a rock, summoning every ounce of strength in my body. I held my breath in suspense.

"I've got you now," his words echoed in my mind and I could hear the smile in his voice. He headed in the direction of my throw and my shoulders slumped in relief. Then he stopped again, my whole body tensing, another thud. Two bodies colliding in the darkness.

All I could make out were grunts, a man desperately fighting to live. Afterward, nothing was there, the noise dissipated in an instant, causing me to wonder if I had just imagined the entire thing. At that moment, a voice interrupted the silence.

"You don't have to do this," he said, his airway constricted, voice full of fear.

It was at that moment that I realized, I was not the one James had been following. It was number fifteen the whole time. My feet moved before I had a chance to think, and I was running towards the danger.

"Of course, I don't have to, but I want to." before James could finish, my elbow collided with his stomach making him grunt. It didn't hit as hard as I hoped, and it probably hurt me more than it hurt him, but it was enough.

As soon as the opportunity came, Fifteen quickly slid away, rising instantly, the surge of adrenaline propelling him forward, yet he did not run. A hand grabbed my wrist, pulling me forward. I resisted with all my strength, but I slid forward anyway. I begged my legs to be stronger, praying that I would make it out alive, but I knew in my very core that it wasn't even a possibility.

In no time at all, James stood right before me, his hot breath burned my eyes, and I was glad for the shadows, glad I could not make out the smile on his face. A loud thud in my ear, which I could only assume was Fifteen, fighting a losing battle and the hand around my wrist let go, setting me free.

I couldn't run, I watched too many people die today and I couldn't stand by and let James claim another victim. So despite the voice in my head, pleading with me to turn around and run, I lurched forward, joining the fight. I took an elbow to the face as Fifteen reared back to punch James. The punch landed, and as James stumbled back, I took the opportunity to kick my foot, right between his legs making him groan.

He grabbed my arm, forcefully this time, raising his knife. Before I could move, he thrust forward, the knife cutting through my thigh. I let out a scream, as my pants became drenched in blood.

He reared back to strike again but fell back when Fifteen shoved him, catching him off guard, and he slipped on the blood of his previous victims. Karma was on my side. I stood there, holding my thigh, trying to stop the bleeding as Fifteen scooped me up in his arms and began running.

For a split second, all I could hear was his heartbeat, echoing in my ears, beating just as fast as my own. But a second later, I heard James get up and run after us, he was getting closer and closer, and Fifteen struggled as my weight slowed him down.

"Leave me," I whispered a sob threatening to break through. "You have to leave me."

"Not a chance in hell," he whispered back through staggered breaths. But James was so close now, we weren't going to make it. There was only one way this was going to end.

We slammed into something, possibly a tree. A whimper broke the silence, followed by a thud and I knew we had run straight into someone else, the force of the hit knocking her down. Fifteen sidestepped to go around her, telling her to run as he passed but didn't slow.

She rushed to stand up, but she couldn't do it in time. James grabbed her, bringing her body toward him and her scream made Fifteen stop in his tracks. She let out another scream, this one gurgling with blood the sound making bile rise in my throat. I knew this would be the last sound that she would ever make.

Fifteen began to run once again, trying to put as much distance between us and James as possible. That should be all though right? Eight dead, the hunt was over, wasn't it? I calculated the numbers again in my head.

In the beginning, I had seen three dead in the clearing, come across three bodies in the woods, then Thirteen, and the girl we just heard die that's eight dead. Unless James never found Thirteen. We had left him there to die, but maybe James never killed him. That would mean that one more would have to die before this was over, and we were the easiest targets.

Fear coiled around my spine and pain reverberated through my leg with every step Fifteen took. I began to shiver, I needed to stop the bleeding. I wiggled in Fifteens' arms, taking my shirt off my body. It was covered in sweat and dirt. Tying it around my leg, I winced as the pain ran up my spine, sending an excruciating sensation I hadn't felt before.

Fifteen slowed and forced us into a bush, the thorns eating away at our skin, but the pain was nothing compared to the aching in my thigh. He had opted for hiding, knowing that James was faster. He gently placed me on the ground and put his finger to my lips, telling me to be quiet as if I was stupid enough to make a sound.

I stopped breathing, forcing my body to be silent, but I knew it was pointless. The thoughts in my mind ran wild, what if they planned on killing all of us? Who's to say they didn't change the rules? They held all the power, so ultimately they could do whatever they wanted. That thought truly terrified me, I was at the mercy of a killer.

After a few seconds, or more likely minutes, my body began to tremble. I witnessed as James appeared, a menacing smile spread across his face. His knife was still dripping with the blood of his latest victim. He looked around, scavenging the area with his eyes until he spotted us, white clothes in a dark forest had given us the disadvantage of the century.

I looked at Fifteen. "You have to run," I whispered in the darkness, but he wasn't looking at me. He stepped forward, towards James.

"Fifteen no, please don't," I begged, and I let the tears fall, already morning the death of this beautiful stranger. My sobs rang in my ears as I watched James get closer and closer. Every step shattering my heart more and more.

James was so close now, and I ripped my eyes from the scene, my heart couldn't take any more pain. I couldn't watch this man die because of me. This was not how this was supposed to go, it was supposed to be me. I was supposed to be the next one dead.

I looked back to see James merely steps from Fifteen, my vision was blurred by the tears. I wanted to throw myself in front of him, to sacrifice my own life to save his. But my knife wound has disintegrated my mobility. I would never get there in time.

So, I did the only thing I could, I shouted out to him "Fifteen run, save yourself. You don't have to be a hero, please just go." I begged which says a lot because I never beg.

"If he wants to hurt you, he'll have to go through me first" There was a darkness in his voice.

"No, please," I sobbed. But it was too late, the killer was already there, standing face-to-face with Fifteen.

Just when I thought all hope was lost, a blinding light appeared, the sudden change making me squint. Confusion took my mind captive and I didn't have time to process it before the intercom spoke

"Congratulations, you have survived level one." That was the last thing I remember before my body seeped farther into the earth and I drifted off to sleep.

Chapter Five

I woke up in a panic, scanning the room with my eyes. I was lying in a bed with white sheets and blankets that blended seamlessly with the white walls. Where was I? Pain throbbed in my leg, making me remember the events leading up to this moment. I closed my eyes, pleading for this not to be real. I had woken from a dream only to find myself living a nightmare.

I sat up to discover, I was dressed in a white shirt and white pants with the occasional smudge of dirt and blood. I slid my pant leg up to discover that my knife wound had been cleaned and stitched up. Confusion drowned my mind as I sat in this bed that wasn't mine.

"Hello?" I uttered a whisper, secretly wishing there was no one around. My voice was raw and quiet, not my own.

I tried again, louder this time "Hello?"

I heard a shuffling noise and flinched as the door swung open. As Fifteen walked in, wearing the same white outfit as me, I couldn't help but smile a little. Tears filled my eyes at the sight of him alive and well.

For the first time, I took a moment to admire his beauty. He has short, fluffy black hair and piercing blue eyes. They are the kind you could get lost in. He has a muscular build, with strong arms, and a welcoming demeanor. And if I'm being honest, his attractiveness is a little intimidating.

"I was beginning to wonder if you were ever going to wake up," he teased.

"What..." I stopped talking realizing nothing else was coming out.

"Here drink some water," he disappeared out the door and came back with a full glass. I downed the whole thing before trying to speak again.

"Thank you," my voice had returned. "What happened? How long have I been asleep? Where are we?" The questions kept forming in my mind. I needed answers, and I needed them now.

"You passed out because you lost too much blood, but we survived the hunt. They separated us and I didn't see you for a while but when they brought you back, they had stitched you up and said you'd be fine. You've been asleep for about a day and a half now. I was really worried," the concern began invading his voice.

"Why would they try to kill me just to stitch me up and save me?" I was asking myself more than I was asking him, but he answered anyway.

"I think they want you healthy for level two, this is all just a big sick game," he tried to mask the distaste in his voice, but his face gave it away.

"What's level two?" Anxiety washed over me, I could not go through that again.

"I don't know," he admitted as his eyes darted to the floor, "but we get a week to recover, we can talk about it more later." He averted his eyes from the floor to me. "You look pale. You should eat something."

My stomach growled at the thought of food, Fifteen handed me the white crutches by the door and I got up, every muscle in my body protesting.

"Oh and one more thing," he said, lowering his voice. "Try to keep the conversations light, some people are not handling things very well."

I nodded my head, the images of the dead bodies resurfacing and suddenly I wasn't so hungry anymore. I peeked my head out the door to find another room, it had a sofa, two love seats, and a TV, everything was white, even the carpet on the floor.

Three people were in this room. An old movie was playing, but nobody was watching it. As we moved forward, everyone was staring at me, but nobody was saying a word.

"Hi," I said feeling awkward. "I'm number three or Amanda I guess."

"I'm Henry, that's Jason and Ashley," he said pointing. I looked at Henry, he looked like the stereotypical nerd. His glasses were too big for his slim face and he had light brown hair that awkwardly hung over a friendly face. He was not conventionally attractive by any means. He was short and skinny but he seemed nice enough.

"Nice to meet you," I said awkwardly.

Then I looked at Jason and gave him a small smile. He has dirty blond hair and a softly shaped jaw with beautiful hazel eyes. He is tall and a little scrawny but overall, a very attractive man. He has a big scar beside his eyebrow that gives him a sense of mystery, and he seems very trustworthy.

Lastly, I looked at Ashley and immediately noticed that she's short, if I had to guess, I'd say she's five foot even. All her features are small, she has a button nose with almond eyes and shoulder-length black hair. She has beautiful golden skin and is easily one of the prettiest girls I've ever seen. Her eyes are puffy and raw like she's been crying for weeks.

"Tristan and Haley are in the kitchen making lunch," Henry continued.

Jason gave me a small wave and Ashley turned back to the TV, pain was emanating from her very soul.

"The kitchen's right through here," Fifteen said, and I followed, the all-white appliances catching my eye. Interrupting her work on the sandwiches, Haley offered me a friendly smile that couldn't quite hide the sadness in her eyes.

"How are you doing? We were all starting to get worried, you slept a long time," she said.

"I'm all right considering," I picked at my nails. "I had hoped all this was a dream."

"Yeah, I thought it was all just a bad dream at first too," Tristan pipped in, "I wish I could tell you it gets easier."

"Well, you should eat, get your strength up," Haley said putting a sandwich on the table, it was obvious she wasn't ready to talk about it.

"Thanks," I mumbled as I sat down.

The first thing I noticed about Haley was her beautiful green eyes which complimented her cool skin tone. She has long blonde hair with natural waves. She's pretty, not in the drop-dead gorgeous type of way but definitely above average. She has kind eyes and a smile that makes you feel safe.

Then I looked at Tristan, He has curly brown hair and honey eyes that compliment his dark skin tone. He is skinny but he has a big frame and is easily six feet tall. He is above average on the attractive scale and his confidence only adds to his charm.

I took a bite of the sandwich and forced myself to swallow. All I could think about was the fact that all those people who died would never eat again. I was overcome with guilt and had to push my plate away, using all my willpower to resist the urge to vomit.

"It gets easier," Fifteen whispered after I pushed the plate away. My confusion vanished and was replaced by rage, as my eyes met his.

"I don't want this to get easier," I closed my eyes for a moment then I began waving my hands around the room, venom in my voice. "People are dead, eight of them. Does that mean nothing to you people? How can you make sandwiches and watch movies like everything is normal? And for the love of God, somebody tell me why everything in this place is white!"

"I meant that eating gets easier, not being in this place," he whispered back, sympathy swelling in his eyes. "We've all been through hell, we can't turn on each other in here, or we won't make it."

"Oh," I whispered back, eyes falling to the floor, "I guess I just need more time to process, I'm sorry." I felt like an idiot, of course, they weren't okay, they were just doing what they needed to do to get through like anyone would. "I'm going to go get cleaned up," I said, getting up.

"The bathroom's right there," Haley said pointing, "The towels are in the top cabinet, and there's a change of clothes in the drawer with your number."

"Okay, thanks," I mumbled, still embarrassed.

"Oh and Three," she said.

I turned around, the number feeling more like my name than Amanda. "Yeah?"

"Everyone had a breakdown on the first day, so don't feel like you have to hold yourself together for our sake," Haley whispered in a voice so low only I could hear.

I nodded, sending her a silent thank you, and walked into the bathroom, using one of my crutches to shut the door.

I took a seat in the shower, the water running down my face, and at that moment I allowed myself to finally cry. I closed my eyes, seeing the terror in Five's eyes as I did, hearing her scream as death pulled her close. Opening my eyes again, the image of her fading, leaving me drowning in the guilt of doing nothing to help her.

I shivered as I remembered thirteen attacking, his sick words, cutting deeper than any knife ever could. My hands instinctively reached for my bruised jaw where his fist collided with bone. The guilt consumed me once again for leaving him there, unconscious, signing his death certificate.

My eyes closed as the tears continued to fall, the lifeless bodies imprinted in my mind for an unending infinity, the screams playing on repeat, daring me to forget the sounds. I sat there until the water turned cold, until there were no more tears left to fall, only then did I get up to scrub off the blood. I scrubbed and scrubbed until I was red and raw, the blood no longer there yet I still felt its presence.

The soap was no match for the uncleanliness in my soul. Even so, I willed the soap to seep into the depths of my skull, to clean even the darkest parts of me, to scrub away the memories that didn't seem to want to leave me be. The memory of what I'd done and the person I'd become.

When I had finally gained the strength to stand, I hobbled out of the shower over to the cabinet with the towels, which to no surprise were all white. I opened the drawer with the number 3 embossed on it and removed an outfit that was an identical match to the one I had woken up in.

I staggered over to the mirror, but my reflection was not my own. The girl looking back at me was not Amanda, but rather a broken fragment of the girl I used to be. I searched the mirror for the fragments of myself still left behind, hoping to find something to cling to, but nothing was there. This wasn't Amanda, this person before me was number three and those two people were not the same.

My hand went to my left eye which was bruised and swollen, only then did I remember Fifteen's elbow making contact with my face. My jaw was swollen, a yellow bruise forming where Thirteen's fist collided with bone. Even in death, his memory continues to mock me.

My face and body were littered with tiny cuts and bruises, from occasional thorns and branches. My flesh was beaten and broken, but my soul was what took the most damage and I feared that this was something I'd never truly be able to recover from.

Worst of all, when I first woke up I had allowed myself to believe that I had been rescued, that this whole thing was over, that I had survived. My heart was wrenched out of my body and thrown into a boxing ring because I allowed myself to have hope. I knew better but I fell for it anyway.

I did survive level one but only to become a victim of level two. I found myself wishing that I hadn't survived at all, then at least this would all be over. I looked at the girl in the mirror one final time before I grabbed my crutches and stumbled out the door.

Chapter Six

I made my way to the living room, where everyone else sat silently staring at nothing, deep in their thoughts no doubt. I shook at the thought, and I wondered if anyone else in this room left someone there to die the way Fifteen and I had. I wondered if anyone sacrificed another life to save their own.

"I know it's getting late but if you're up for it, we can play a game?" Fifteen asked, in a whisper making me wonder if the room was bugged and someone was listening.

I answered with a hushed, "Okay," as I glanced around the room for cameras. Nothing seemed out of the ordinary, so I sat beside him. "What are we playing?"

"Maybe instead of a game, we can just tell each other a little bit about ourselves," Tristan suggested.

"That's a good idea, who wants to go first?" Jason asked.

"This might be stupid but what if we narrowed it down a little more, like asking specific questions and everyone can answer? Because nobody knows what to say when someone says tell me about yourself," I said, this whole thing seeming so dumb. But what was I supposed to do after seeing so many people killed in cold blood? I had no clue.

Jason let out a small laugh "Yeah you're right, you wanna come up with the questions?" He asked, his eyes pinning me to the couch.

I'd rather do literally anything else, but that's not what I said. "Sure unless someone else wants to?" I asked and everyone shook their heads, sealing me to my fate. "Alright, umm... why don't we start with something simple? Favorite color?" I asked.

"Mine's dark blue," Fifteen said.

"Green," said Jason and Haley, another blue from Tristan.

"Mine's black, I know it's a shade, not a color, but I've always liked black," I said, not realizing how emo it sounded until after it came out.

"My favorite color used to be red," Henry trailed off, his eyes falling to the floor. "But now it reminds me of the blood..." He paused, "there was so much blood." He gulped, the sound echoing in the silent room.

Don't think about it, don't think about it.

I repeated it again and again in my mind, but the image still seeped through, blurring my vision. The bodies, the pools of blood, it was all too much for my broken heart to handle.

"What about you, Ashley?" Fifteen spoke, ripping me from my thoughts, for which I'd be eternally grateful.

Silence followed. Ashley was still staring at the wall and it was apparent that her mind was unwilling to return to her body. A single tear streamed down her cheek. What had she seen?

"Okay, next question," Tristan spoke, silently telling us to leave Ashley alone.

"Umm, who's most likely looking for you right now?" I asked hoping for rescue.

"My girlfriend thinks I'm participating in a clinical trial for six months," Fifteen leaned back, putting his hands behind his head. For some reason, I couldn't quite figure out, my heart sank in my chest.

Nobody else had people who would notice their absence and I hardly believed it was a coincidence. We were societal rejects, foster kids, homeless, or children of junkies. If anything we'd be labeled as runaways. We had little to no shot of being found, especially if nobody was looking for us.

"Wait, a clinical trial?" I asked, my mind putting the pieces together. "I signed up for a clinical trial too."

"So did I," Tristan said meeting my eyes.

"So everyone in this room signed up for a clinical trial?" I asked, and they all nodded except Ashley who continued to stare blankly at the wall.

"So this is the clinical trial? The brochure said you could leave at any time, but we're being held against our will, so it doesn't make sense." Haley rose from her seat and began pacing the room.

"Was this all just fabricated to see how we'd react?" I asked.

"There's no way. Those people actually died, I saw it happen. Whatever this is, it's real," Jason said.

"Maybe the money for participating in the trial was just a way to draw people in?" Tristan asked.

"They're smart," I said thinking out loud. "They found a way to ensure nobody would be looking for us for a long time." I paused, "we fell for it."

At that instant, just one idea resounded in my brain, one so dark I would never dare express it. No matter what I tried to do to take my mind off of it, the thought stubbornly refused to leave. *Not a single one of us was going to make it out of this place alive.*

"It's late, we should all get going to bed," Haley said, stifling a yawn as she forced the conversation to an end. She didn't seem to want to talk about any of this, it was as if she was living in a state of denial. I couldn't blame her though, denial is so much better than this reality.

"Yeah it's about that time," Tristan responded getting up from the couch.

Everyone said goodnight, going to their separate rooms leaving just me, Fifteen, and Ashley in the living room.

"Hey I've got some questions, I didn't ask earlier because I didn't want to scare anyone. Can we talk?" I spoke in a whisper.

He let out a humorless laugh, "I think we've all got a lot of questions and not a lot of answers, but I'll answer what I can. What do you want to know?" Fifteen whispered back, running his hands through his coal-colored hair.

I held up a finger telling him to wait a second and I went over to Ashley.

"Hi, I know this is an awful situation and this is a stupid question but are you okay?" My words were uttered in a quiet, calming tone. She didn't move, speak, or even acknowledge my presence.

"Okay, you don't have to speak until you're ready, just know I'm here if you ever need to talk to someone. Me and Fifteen are going to help you to bed okay?" Complete and total silence followed.

I motioned to Fifteen, and he carried Ashley to bed, I covered her with a blanket and set a bottle of water beside her bed. It didn't take a doctor to know that there was something seriously wrong and I wished there was something, anything I could do to help her.

GAMES OF RUIN

I followed Fifteen back to the living room and turned on a movie to fill the silence. "I'm worried about her," I whispered.

"I am too," Fifteen said, "she's been like that all day, hopefully she'll be herself again in the morning but all we can do right now is wait." He was right, I knew he was, but I was still worried.

"Waiting is a nightmare," I whispered then changed the subject, "so earlier you said someone told you I'd be fine who were you referring to? Was it James?" As I said it, the name tasted bitter on my lips.

"No, God no. It was a doctor I think, she was wearing scrubs, and she brought you in while you were still unconscious. Me and Tristan put you in bed, and she left."

"So, there are two of them?"

"At least," he said, "but by the look of this place, I'd say there's a whole lot more."

I felt panic clawing up my body and goosebumps overtook my skin "Tell me everything from the moment I passed out. Don't leave out a single detail," I pleaded.

"Sure, I can do that, but do you mind telling me why?" Why does any of it even matter?" He asked, plopping his face into his hands in defeat.

"Because we need to come up with a way to get the hell out of here," I whispered desperately.

He nodded his head in understanding. "They announced the hunt was over, and the lights came on, the sun was back in the sky."

"That doesn't make sense, it was the middle of the night," I interrupted.

"Yeah, it turns out we were never really outside, the sun, moon, temperature, clouds, and everything were all fake. Anyway, that's beside the point. I carried you to the clearing where the hunt started, and the nurse took you away, she said she'd save you. There was a bin with blindfolds and James told us to put them on. We didn't want to, but he threatened to kill us," he looked down at the floor, ashamed, and I hated myself for even making him share. "He handcuffed us all to this metal bar and led us to this room." He finally met my eyes.

I scooted closer, in an attempt to comfort his wounded soul, wishing I could dismember his sadness, piece by piece.

"Did you keep track of the turns you took to get here? Do you know if you were inside or outside or if you went through any doors or anything that might help us get out?" I spoke in a whisper.

"Honestly not really, I was worried about you, and I was pretty sure I was getting led to my death, so I wasn't really paying attention." He slid a hand through his hair again, it was a gesture he seemed to do often.

"Right, sorry," I mumbled.

"I know we walked for a while before we got here, and I know it was indoors because of the air conditioning. There were a lot of turns and a lot of doors, the doors make a buzzing noise when they're opened." He began retorting the information fast like he had been over it a thousand times in his head. "Either they led us around in circles, or this place is massive."

He reached his hand up to my face, stroking just below my eye, making my heart stop." Forgive me?" he asked, dropping his hand.

"What?" I asked confusion running around in my mind, making me dizzy.

"I elbowed you in the face, I hate myself for hurting you," he whispered as his eyes fell to the floor once again.

"It doesn't even hurt," I flashed him a fake smile, hoping he couldn't see through my facade.

"You're a bad liar," he smiled. "I never got to thank you."

"For what, almost getting you killed?"

"Shut up," he rolled his eyes. "I'd be dead right now if it wasn't for you."

"Back at ya," I replied with a small laugh.

The room fell into a soft silence, neither of us knew what to say to the other. We had gone through a living nightmare and our relationship would be everlasting because of it.

I flinched when he finally spoke, "We should try and get some sleep, but I'll see you in the morning," he said, rising from the couch.

"Okay, Night," I muttered, heading towards my door.

"Goodnight Amanda," he said, my name sounding so much more beautiful coming out of his mouth.

"It's not though, just a night, not a good one," I jokingly remarked, downplaying the heart-wrenching circumstances.

"You always seem to have something to say, don't you?" He teased, "Maybe your dreams will take you to a better place, maybe you will have a good night, even if it isn't real" With that, he leaned against his doorway.

"Hey, just one more question," I grinned.

"What?" He asked, a twinkle in his eyes as he rolled them.

"What's your name?"

He paused with a mischievous grin on his face, "Wouldn't you like to know?" He murmured before entering the room labeled 15.

Chapter Seven

I let out a shaky breath as I entered my room, the terror of being alone crept into the back of my mind, threatening to make me panic. I flipped the light on. The terror slightly subsided, and I climbed into bed, pulling up the covers, to shield myself from this awful world.

I closed my eyes to only immediately open them again, the images of death ingrained in the hard drive of my mind. The fear in Fives' eyes and the desperation in her screams were all waiting to arise the moment my eyes closed. So I lay there, my eyes not daring to shut, my mind on constant overdrive, trying to think about anything else.

Was I really safe in this room? Who's to say that James won't come in here while I'm sleeping? The thought terrified me and I wished so desperately that I wasn't in here alone. I thought of sleeping in someone else's room, just to have the company but I didn't know these people and I wanted to give them space.

So, instead, I opted to hide under the blanket and pretend this wasn't real. Maybe Haley was onto something with the whole denial thing.

A loud knock sounded on my door and my whole body tensed, fearing for the worst.

"Amanda, It's Haley, can I come in?"

"Yeah," I said, sitting up and she opened the door.

"I can't sleep, I keep seeing the blood and all those people dead." She started to silently sob, "It was... it was so awful, Amanda. I don't... I don't think I can be alone."

"Hey, it's okay," I got up and pulled her into a hug "I don't really want to be alone either, every time I close my eyes, it hurts. It hurts to see them limp, and not breathing, it hurts to hear their screams." My eyes threatened to tear up, but I didn't allow it. "Do you want to sleep in here with me tonight?" I silently prayed her answer was yes.

"Yeah, I'm sorry," she wiped the tears from her eyes "I just don't want to be alone"

"Me either," I whispered as we laid down in my bed.

"I don't want to talk, I just want to-"

"It's okay, we don't have to," I interrupted. "Let's just go to sleep, and if you change your mind or need anything I'm here okay?"

A somber silence fell.

"Hey Amanda?"

"Yeah?"

She stared wistfully at me. "Thank you".

"We're in this together Haley, you don't have to thank me,"

After that, the silence returned. I must have laid there for hours until my body finally drifted to sleep. Haley's sobs served as my only lullaby.

I hadn't been asleep for long when I awoke in a panic, startled by a loud crack that rang in my ears. My feet hit the floor in an instant, my hands raising, preparing to fight. I scanned the room only to find nothing out of place, Haley was just as startled as me.

GAMES OF RUIN

I got halfway to my door to check on the others before a voice came over the intercom, making me freeze in my tracks.

"You'll find blindfolds on the kitchen table, put them on, and wait for further instruction," the intercom crackled off. I opened my door, joining the others in the kitchen.

"What happens if we don't?" I asked, feeling the bitter taste of fear on my tongue.

"We die," Tristan said, trying to mask the terror in his voice.

"It's going to be okay, let's just do what they say," my eyes fell to the floor.

Ashley whimpered behind me "I can't, I can't do whatever this is." I glanced back as her tears began to fall at a rapid rate.

I had no time to be grateful, that she had come out of shock "You can Ashley, we'll all be together, we don't have a choice".

"They said we had a week until level two." Jason shouted, making us all jump, "How is this fair?"

"It's not, but we have to do what we're told," Fifteen said, taking charge.

Opting to feel hopeful rather than terrified, Tristan said, "Maybe they're letting us go."

The intercom crackled "This is your one warning, put on your blindfolds, or we will host another hunt."

We exchanged apprehensive glances, our eyes wide with fear. We all drew our blindfolds over our eyes without uttering a single word.

"Now what?" Haley voiced her thoughts.

Chapter Eight

Nobody had time to answer before we heard the door buzz, and then swing open. Strong hands cuffed us to a metal pole, one by one. My whole body shook, the tension in the room made it hard to breathe.

Were we in this room with James, the man who hunted us and killed some of our own? Or was it someone entirely different, someone with unique horrors to teach us? I didn't know which was worse.

We began to move in an uncoordinated line, bumping into each other, speeding up and slowing down. I did my best to memorize the way, my mind welcoming the distraction but before long, we came to a crashing halt, half of us almost falling to the floor.

The handcuffs were taken off, but I didn't dare move, the silence in the room was deafening. The buzzing of the door made me finch, but as soon as I heard it close, I ripped the blindfold off.

The light stung my eyes, but even so, I whipped my head around to take in my surroundings. I recognized this place, I had been here before. The room resembled a small theater, it had several folding seats with a TV that took up an entire wall.

A sense of relief was evident in Jason's voice, "It's just the initiation room."

"The what?" Fifteen asked, but before Jason could answer, the lights in the room dimmed and the TV roared to life. Sitting in our seats, we all had our eyes fixed on the screen.

"Congratulations on completing level one" the voice was automated. "This is the initiation room where you will come every week to get your clue for the next level. You will also hear tips from others who have completed the level you are on. If you understand, please say continue."

"Continue," Fifteen said, tension fuming in his voice.

"This week's clue is water." The screen changed from a blank screen to a girl, her head underwater. She was drowning, we watched as the life slowly drained from her eyes. I forced myself to look away, I couldn't keep watching people die. Anger began to fuse in the pit of my stomach. How could people be so cruel?

Then the screen changed once again, to a different girl. Her hair was dripping with water and her voice shook with every word "Don't panic, that's the only advice I can give you, stay calm or people will end up dead." The blank screen returned, but the image of the girl drowning remained imprinted in my mind, where it would forever reside.

"If you understand, please say continue," the TV spoke.

Tristan rose from his seat, "No I don't freaking understand" he shouted, a little too loud making me flinch. "I don't understand any of it. Why are you doing this? Let us go."

"If you want to rewatch the clip, say replay."

My heart sank, seeing that girl drown once was heartbreaking. I didn't have it in me to see it again. "Continue," I said, clutching the armrest.

GAMES OF RUIN

Tristan sat back down, defeated. There was nothing we could do to get ourselves out of this mess. None of us wanted to admit it but deep down, we all knew we were doomed.

"This week requires a selection, when your name is stated, please pick a number between 1 and 7."

Acting on the instructions we had been given, we selected our numbers.

"Thank you for your cooperation, the order is as follows: Ashley, Jason, Matthew (Fifteen), Haley, Henry, Amanda, Tristan."

I exchanged a look with Fifteen, his eyes were wild with fear, directly reflecting my own.

"You have four days until level two, Good luck." The TV shut off, and the lights turned back on, but nobody stood up. The fear was like an invisible weight pressing us down, one that couldn't be lifted. There was only one thing I knew for sure, we've seen their faces and witnessed their crimes. *These people have no intention of letting us go.*

The intercom cracked on, telling us to put our blindfolds on, and of course, we had no choice but to comply. The same strong hands that brought us into the room also assisted in our exit and I tried to convince myself that it was anyone but James.

Even still, his presence haunted me. I did my very best to memorize the turns and doors we went through although it was probably pointless, I'm sure I'll be killed in level 2. The map in my mind may never get used but I still had to try. Before long, we were back in our room.

Chapter Nine

I yanked off my blindfold the moment I heard the door shut.

"We're going to die," Ashley spoke in a low voice, and I was concerned that she wouldn't even make it to level two, that the fear would kill her first.

"No," Jason said "We just have to figure this out, we have four days, we can figure this out together."

I disregarded everyone else and walked to the whiteboard near the TV and picked up the dry-erase marker near it.

"What are you doing?" Haley questioned me as if I had lost my mind.

"I need to write down everything I know so far, so I can figure this thing out."

She gave a slight nod.

"I agree, we should find out what everyone knows and write it down. But first..." Fifteen said, "How did you know what that room was?" He questioned, his gaze fixed accusingly on Jason.

"Because I was one of the first ones here!" He replied in a defensive tone.

"It was where we were briefed on level one," I said, "Numbers 1-10 got briefed, but 11-15 didn't. They didn't capture us all at the same time, some of us got to prepare for the hunt." As if that's even something you could prepare for, I thought, keeping that part to myself.

"So who got here first?" Fifteen posed the question, still trying to make sense of it.

"I was," I said, "I'm Three, One and Two... didn't make it" The images of their bodies piled in the woods flashed through my mind, and I had to fight back the tears threatening to fall.

"So you were held here?" Fifteen surveyed the surroundings questioningly.

"Nah, it was a different room," Jason said "but everyone wasn't there. It was just me, Tristan, and one other guy."

"I was with One and Two, we were in a room with a dirt floor, it was kind of like a dungeon," I said, "but I was here at least a whole week before the hunt"

"Do you remember what happened when you were in the initiation room the first time? Did they tell you why they're doing this?" Haley asked.

"No, it was even less information than this time," Henry said.

"They told us there would be a hunt in five days, that half of us would be killed. Then they gave us the rules and that was it," Tristan added.

"What were the rules?" Haley asked.

"The rules were that we couldn't kill the hunter and couldn't kill each other, or we'd be eliminated," I started waving the marker, "can we start writing things down now?"

"Yeah, yeah okay," Fifteen said, and I began to write.

Level 2
Hint: Water
Image: Drowning

GAMES OF RUIN

Tip: Stay calm
Order: Ashley, Jason, Fifteen, Haley, Henry, Amanda, Tristan
Overall

- **Other people were/are in the same situation.**

- **Substantial amounts of time and money were invested in creating this prison.**

- **No one is looking for us**

"Is there anything else we should add?" I asked.
Everyone shook their heads.
"Maybe the next time someone comes to take us to another room, we attack them and break out?" Tristan suggested.
"Attack them with what?" Ashley said. "The knives, plates, and bowls are all plastic, anything we could use as a weapon is secured to the floor. They planned this and when they did, they made sure we couldn't use anything against them." None of us wanted to admit it, but she had a point.
"She's right," Haley said.
"Well, why do we even need a weapon?" Jason asked. "It would be 7 against what like one or two? We could easily take them."
"Yeah, yeah he's right," Tristan said as hope engulfed his voice.
"But what about the doors?" I asked, "They're all locked, and we don't have a code if there even is a co-" My voice faded into nothingness as I heard the crack of the intercom.

"Any attempt to escape, or hurt any of us will result in another hunt." The voice hissed and the intercom shut off.

Ashley began to cry, the sound exploded as if it had been trapped in for far too long. Haley rushed to soothe her, wrapping her in a big hug. As if her arms could somehow shield her from this hell. My eyes locked with Fifteen's, an understanding hanging in the balance.

They were listening.

Chapter Ten

"I think I'm going to be sick," I said, covering my mouth and running to the bathroom. After a second I said, "Fifteen will you come here and hold my hair back".

There was no verbal reply, but the sound of feet walking towards me was the only response I needed. As soon as he walked into the bathroom, he started to draw my hair back as if he'd done it thousands of times.

I stood up and pushed his hands away, the motion making his eyebrows pull together in confusion. I switched on the shower and without hesitation, I dragged him in with me.

"Slow your role," he said, a smirk tugging at his lips "I'm all for spontaneity, but I do have a girlfriend."

"Shut up," I said trying to hide the smile forming on my lips. I rolled my eyes "cocky doesn't suit you."

"Liar," he said with a chuckle.

"I thought it would be better to chat here, away from prying ears," I spoke, moving on to a new topic.

"Why can't we just find the bugs and destroy them?"

"Because there would be no guarantee that we'd be able to find them all, and we'd probably be punished," I hissed.

"So how do we know we're not being watched too? If we are, they'll know exactly what we're doing. It's not every day you see two people take a shower with all their clothes on."

He asked, and it caught me off guard. The thought made me nauseous. Of course, they were watching, I don't know why I hadn't considered that earlier.

"Is that your way of trying to get me to take my clothes off?" I teased, making light of a bad situation. "Because really until a couple of minutes ago, I didn't even know your name. You don't waste any time do you?"

"Don't threaten me with a good time," he laughed with a hunger in his eyes. "trust me, if I wanted you to take your clothes off, you'd know." He took a step towards me, pinning me to the wall.

"You sure about that?" I looked up at him and the world fell away.

"Positive," he whispered, then took a step back. "But like I mentioned, I'm off the market."

I composed myself, "So I've heard. Wait, what you said earlier about being watched, I have an idea," I said, turning the shower off. We dried off and walked out the bathroom door, without so much as another word.

"Are you okay?" Haley asked as I stepped out of the bathroom. Then her expression shifted when she saw Fifteen walking out behind me, his hair just as wet as mine.

"Nice job, man," Jason said, patting Fifteen on the back.

"Gross," I groaned, "it's not like that."

"Gross? Ouch," Fifteen winced.

"Do you need a carpenter?" Tristan asked, looking at Fifteen.

"A carpenter?" Fifteen's eyebrows pulled together.

"To rebuild the ego Amanda just demolished," Tristan said, making everyone laugh, except for Ashley.

GAMES OF RUIN

"Alright guys," Fifteen chuckled.

"How can you make jokes and laugh at a time like this?" Ashley was still trying to get the tears to stop falling. "We were kidnapped and hunted. Soon we'll have to do level two, which some of us might not survive, there's nothing funny about that."

"No there's not," Tristan said, his voice low, "but if we can't laugh and make jokes then I won't be able to survive. Humor is the only thing that can stop me from losing my sanity in a place like this, and I will be destroyed without it. So yes I understand the situation we're in. And yes I'm just as scared and sad as you Ashley, but if those are the only two emotions I allow myself to feel what kind of life is that?"

"He's right Ash," I said, "we're not trying to be insensitive, we're all just having a really hard time and everyone copes in different ways. We're all just doing what we have to do to survive."

"I'm sorry. I didn't see it that way," Ashley said, wiping a tear from her eye.

"I know what I'm about to do is crazy but just trust me and don't say a word," I said, altering the conversation. Then I walked to the kitchen, grabbed some tinfoil, crushed it into a ball, and put it in the microwave.

"What on earth are you doing?" Fifteen propelled himself forward.

"Shh," I turned around, "Do you trust me?"

"I don't know you," he said, avoiding my gaze.

"You know me." My eyes met his and it was a clash of ice and fire.

"I won't allow you to put yourself in a situation where you're going to get yourself hurt," he said.

"You won't allow me to?" I laughed without humor, "Did I travel back in time? Last I checked, I live in a world where women are allowed to make their own decisions."

"Last I checked, we were no longer bound to the rules of a governed society." He growled, pinning my body to the wall in one swift motion.

My heart caught in my throat and my body forgot how to exhale. I opened my mouth to speak but no words came out.

"Hello? Did you guys forget you're not the only two people in existence?" Tristan asked and Fifteen let me go.

I struggled to stand on my wobbling legs but I reached up to whisper in his ear. "I'm not going to put myself in danger, I promise".

"I guess they did," Jason laughed.

I walked to the microwave and began to input a time.

The intercom cracked on. "Causing an explosion will result in another hunt," it spat.

"Do you have a death wish?" Tristan asked taking the tinfoil out of the microwave.

"Do you want me to lie and say no?"

Tristan blinked slowly at me.

I walked back to the bathroom, put the plug in the bathtub, and turned on the faucet. The others trailed in my footsteps, suspecting I had gone insane.

Chapter Eleven

"Now we know they're not just listening, but they're watching us too," Fifteen whispered.

"Exactly," I said, grateful he understood.

"I understand that the water will hide our voices but why are you filling up the tub?" Haley searched my face for an answer.

"I want to know if there's a camera in here too."

"I've been naked in here," Haley said, disgust flooding her voice.

"We all have," Jason said a little too loud.

"Go back out there and act like everything's normal," I said. "I'm going to overflow the tub, just don't say anything about it."

Despite their lingering doubts, they ended up leaving the room and I closed the door. As the tub filled, it began to overflow, and it wasn't long before the bathroom was filled with water.

I expected to hear the crack of the intercom, but it didn't come. The water trickled beneath the bathroom door, infiltrating the living room before the dreaded sound filled my ears.

Crack. "Turn off the faucet and clean up the water. I will not give you another warning today."

A wave of relief washed through me as I rushed to shut off the faucet. Everyone came over to help clean up the mess, and the mood of the group was slightly elevated. The rest of the place might be monitored but at least the bathroom was our own. We now had a safe space.

The next few days dragged on, the anticipation of level two weighing heavy on our souls. None of us were getting much sleep, we were trying to crack an unsolvable riddle, and our only clue was water. There was something about the uncertainty that made it all the more unbearable.

Now, with the threat of level two only hours away, our spirits were down to unthinkable levels. Everyone had an unmistakable fear in their eyes, recognizing that these few hours could be our final ones. I was pacing around the room, staring at the whiteboard as if it might suddenly give us another clue.

"Stop pacing," Fifteen said. "You're stressing everyone out."

"I can't help it," I said sitting by his side. "We're missing something, we have to be."

"I don't think we're going to figure it out," Jason snapped "We've been at it for days, It's time to let it go".

"He's right," Haley whispered, sympathy dancing in her eyes. "We need to eat, get our strength up. It's all we can do to prepare."

Haley and Tristan had taken up cooking, it was their role, what they needed to do to keep from going insane. Ashley was filled with fear and her tears never stopped, she spent the majority of her days in bed.

Jason's fury was more apparent than his sorrow, he would often yell or snap, but he could also make you laugh, despite all odds. Henry was the quiet one, the one who often stayed alone in his room.

I was the problem solver, the one everyone counted on to get them out of this mess. I was the one consumed by uncovering what level two entailed. Fifteen was the glue that held the group together, the natural leader.

We all had our roles to play, and I was substantially failing at mine.

Tristan and Haley served us breakfast, and the whole group took their seats at the table. We weren't hungry, yet we ate bite after bite, attempting to ignore the fact that this could be our last meal.

"I know we don't know each other very well," I said staring at the wall, "but you guys have become pretty important to me" I cleared my throat.

Haley came over and engulfed me in a tight hug. "We're all going to make it, it'll be okay," everything in my body wanted to believe her. I couldn't figure out why, but I felt a strong urge to keep her safe no matter what.

"She's right, I'm like unreasonably attached to all of you," Ashley laughed through tears. "I guess trauma has a way of bringing people together."

"I hate the circumstances, but I'm so glad I met all of you," Tristan said looking at me.

"Okay guys," Jason said. "No need to get mushy, this isn't a goodbye." His voice was serious, and it made us all laugh.

For a moment, just a few quick seconds, I had forgotten the pain, the torture, and the trauma. It was just me and these people who had quickly become my friends. But like all good moments, it abruptly came to an end, and I was dragged back down to my own personal hell.

Chapter Twelve

We hadn't even finished eating when we heard the dreaded crack of the intercom, telling us to put on our blindfolds. Ashley's sobbing filled the room, a sound we knew all too well. Jason began to yell, another sound not foreign to our ears.

Tristan and Haley glanced at one another for reassurance and Henry's eyes filled with fear. Panic clawed at my throat, making it hard to breathe.

Fifteen grabbed the blindfolds and passed them out, his posture cold and unwelcoming. He was doing this as a way of preparing himself for what was coming, in the same way I transitioned from Amanda to number three. The two might have shared a body, but we were not even close to the same person.

Taking control of the situation, Fifteen said, "We have to put them on; we can't risk making them angry. It's going to be fine, just remember to stay calm. Whatever this is, we'll get through it together." His speech sounded comforting yet distant, I knew on the inside he was just as terrified as I was.

"See you on the other side," Tristan said as he pulled the blindfold over his eyes. We all did the same, no one said another word, and the only noise left in the room was Ashley's quiet sobs.

Seconds trickled away, and then minutes. I stood in the dark, alone and afraid, my heartbeat in my ears, anticipation haunting my soul. I felt overwhelmed by the silence, and the floor seemed to be crumbling away beneath me, dragging me down.

Panic was gripping my chest, squeezing harder and harder with each passing moment, it physically hurt to breathe. Something wasn't right, they never took this long to get us. My whole body was pleading with me to remove the blindfold and get my vision back. I began to spiral, the battle between panic and sanity was over and panic had won.

I felt something touch my arm, I flinched hard, willing it to go away, but it didn't. Someone's hand felt around for mine, I wrapped my fingers around theirs, the panic slightly subsiding. I heard the door buzzing open and at that moment I was no longer Amanda, I was number three.

When we got to the room and ripped our blindfolds off, there was a man dressed in all black, a knife strapped to his side. He instructed us to have a seat, and we all did as we were told.

"Now, I just want to start by saying that everyone can survive this level," he said, and a weight was lifted off my chest "However, with that being said if you make one mistake, or take too long, people will die." The weight returned, threatening to crush every inch of me.

"Today you will be bobbing for apples," he said a smile forming on his lips. "In these apples, there's a key that unlocks the next person's cage. Your order was decided at initiation, Ashley will go first and Tristan will go last," he paused for effect. My face drained of blood.

GAMES OF RUIN

I was next to last, this could be my last few moments alive. But I couldn't think like that, I was number three not Amanda, and I had no time for fear. I looked over at Tristan, his eyes a direct reflection of the fear in his soul. He had his whole life ahead of him, I couldn't sit back and let him die.

"I want to go last." Without pausing to consider, I spoke and everyone's gaze felt like it could cut through me.

"Amanda don't do this," Fifteen commanded, his eyes dark and cold.

I ignored him, looking only at the one in charge "Let me swap places with Tristan," I said, my voice sounding bolder than I felt.

"The order was decided at initiation, you can't trade places," he said with amusement in his voice.

"Why can't I trade places with him? Aren't you going to enjoy the show no matter who dies?" I spat, almost impressed with the bravery number three possessed, it certainly wasn't a quality of Amanda's.

"I said no, if you speak again, we will host another hunt, and half of you will die. Is that what you want?" He asked. I sadly shook my head and slumped back into my seat. I was powerless in this place, just another toy for them to play with and I hated every moment of it.

I cast Tristan another glance, wordlessly conveying my apology. Then the man in charge led us to an adjacent room with seven empty tanks, each of them around 7 feet tall.

"You will have just enough time for everyone to live, but one mistake and someone will die. The rules are simple, retrieve the apple using only your mouth. When you get out of the cage, you are permitted to use your hands to get the key out of the apple and unlock the next cage." He paused for a breath and the silence stung my ears. "The first cage will be unlocked," his eyes shifted to Ashley. "You have to wait for the buzzer before you retrieve the apple. The last cage will have an apple with a prize inside. If you survive," he looked at Tristan, "you get to keep the prize."

"Lucky me," Tristan mumbled.

"If you break the rules at any point or refuse to play, you will be disqualified. Do you have any questions?"

"When you say disqualified, what does that m-mean?" Haley asked, the fear apparent in her voice.

"We'll kill you, anyone else?" We all shook our heads in unison. "Then let's get started, everyone get in your tanks," he barked. I walked over to my tank and got inside, the apple beside my feet. I kept my eyes low, not wanting to see the fear in anyone's eyes, not wanting them to see the fear in mine.

"Hey, guys?" Tristan said, his confidence catching me off guard. "If you let me die I'm going to haunt you." He let out a humorless laugh.

"No one's going to let you die," Fifteen said despite the fact that it ultimately wasn't up to him.

Then Tristan whispered to me in a voice so low, that only I could hear it.

"Amanda," he said.

The name didn't register.

"Amanda," he said again, more forcefully.

That time, it dragged me from my thoughts "Yeah?" I asked, looking him in the eye.

"If I don't make it"

"Don't talk like that Tristan," I shook my head.

GAMES OF RUIN

"Shh, just let me finish. If I don't make it, tell my brother I said Lego."

"What?" I asked. I was growing more nervous by the second.

"Lego, he'll get it."

"Tell him yourself," I said. "This isn't the end."

"Just promise me, Amanda," he pleaded.

"Fine, I promise but you have to do something for me too," I said, proposing a compromise.

"What could I possibly do for you?" he laughed without humor.

"When you feel like giving up, when you don't think you can survive any longer, you think of your brother and you fight. You fight with all you have so that one day you'll see him again."

"Deal," he said, and with that, the time for conversation was over.

The man in charge went around each tank, locking all the tops except Ashley's. Then he gave a thumbs up to a camera and the tanks began filling with water.

Chapter Thirteen

The water was so hot that it felt like fire, and I quickly clambered up the tank to avoid being burned. The water rose so slowly that the anticipation twisted my insides. The steam of the water had completely clouded my tank and sweat was rolling down my back.

It was getting hard to breathe, and I was starting to panic. Hyperventilation had become my best friend, introducing me to anxiety and heart palpitations. But I needed to get a grip, the tank was nearly halfway full now, and I wouldn't be able to avoid the scorching water for long.

I needed a distraction, I needed to think of literally anything else.

I thought back to my early childhood before my life unraveled, I thought of playing hide and seek with my younger sister in that house on top of the hill. I always let her win, hiding in the easiest of places, but her laugh always made me feel like I had somehow won too.

The shrill sound of the buzzer ripped me away from my sanctuary and forced me back into the depths of hell. I reached a free hand out and wiped a spot on the tank so I could see as Ashley struggled to get the apple in her mouth, her face a mix of agony and concentration.

KJ RIVERS

The water had picked up now, filling the tank faster and I could no longer avoid it. The smoldering water reached me, immediately coating my body in pink splotches. In a desperate attempt to keep my cries from escaping, I bit my tongue, yet my body still betrayed me with a distressed whimper. My entire body shriveled in pain, the water felt like a blazing inferno from the depths of hell.

I heard a few other screams and instantly knew that the water had reached my friends as well. My whole body was screaming, the pain was nearly too much to bear, but I didn't want anyone to hear the terror in my screams. So, I shut my mouth tight, biting my tongue to stay quiet.

Tears welled up in my eyes due to the excruciating pain, yet I refused to let them fall. Rather than show my hurt, I glanced upwards, gazed into the lens of the camera, and defiantly waved my middle finger. "Go to hell," I whispered.

In just a few seconds, I'd be out of air, but the pain was such a distraction that I didn't have time to panic. My eyes were glued to Ashley who had gotten out of her tank and was unlocking Jason's, her hands fumbling with the keys. I took one final breath and shut my eyes before the water completely consumed the tank.

I began searching for the apple, trying to ignore the pain of the inferno that engulfed my entire body. I swam up the tank, only stopping when my head hit the top. Then I swam until my face hit something, I pushed the apple up against the side of the tank and after several attempts, finally got it in my mouth. I bit down hard until my teeth were stuck in its juicy core.

I felt something wrap around my neck, and I had to force my eyes to stay closed. I let my hands explore the object, a wave of relief washing over me when I discovered it was a pair of goggles. I quickly put them on and opened my eyes, the world was spinning on its axis, partially from the intense heat and partially from the lack of oxygen.

As soon as my eyes adjusted, I found both Ashley and Jason's tanks empty. Jason was pulling Fifteen from his tank, shouting words I could not hear. My oxygen was running out, and my lungs were burning with deprivation. I willed Fifteen to move faster, but I couldn't stand to look any longer.

I turned my face to look at Tristan, but there was something different about him now. Survival had overtaken fear and his eyes were wild with emotion. He was going to die in this tank, and he knew it, we all did. Tears welled up in my eyes and I looked back to Fifteen.

My lungs were howling for air, there was no way I was going to survive. The stinging of the water was no longer a distraction, it was instead aiding and abetting my panic, tightening around my chest.

My eyes followed Haley, her body as red as mine felt. I saw the panic in her strides, the fate of her friends in her hands. She was nearly halfway to Henry when she fumbled.

I saw it happen in slow motion, the water on the floor mixed with the pain in her steps. It was bound to happen, she slipped and fell, sending the key flying. The last thing I remember was her frantically scrambling towards the key, that's when I lost all consciousness.

My body lay limp, floating to the top of the tank, but that's not where my mind continued to reside.

Chapter Fourteen

I was working my part-time job, back home, this included putting books on shelves and chatting with customers. It appeared to be an average day on the surface, yet something felt off. My customers looked familiar, like I somehow knew these strangers but of course, that was impossible.

Something else was different too, all the walls in the library were white, when did management decide to paint the walls? Why was the white so suffocating? Slowly, all the books, tables, and even the plant at the desk were turning white, I looked down at my clothes as the vibrant red uniform was eaten away and replaced with white.

Confusion prickled at my brain, urging me to solve the problem, to fix what was broken. But the coloration of my world was not the only thing amiss. The air conditioner must have broken because the room was getting hotter and hotter.

But that didn't make a lot of sense either as the temperature shouldn't be climbing so quickly. My mind began to spin, panic threatening to seep through my expanding pores.

I looked around as people whispered in hushed tones, something normal in a library, but today it felt different, sneakier. Nobody seemed to notice that everything was white or that the temperature was beginning to hurt, like being imprinted in the sun.

"I have to get out of here," I shouted aloud and everyone in the library stopped to stare at me like I was the crazy one.

Someone reached out and grabbed my wrist. "You're not going anywhere," he said with a creepy grin overtaking his lips.

"Where did you even come from?" I asked with a shaky voice, "let me go."

I broke my hand away and ran to the door.

"I wouldn't do that if I were you," the creepy stranger warned.

"Well, you're not me, are you?"

I had to get away, so I ignored his advice and found myself yanking the door open. I immediately wanted to take it back. A cascade of water rushed towards me, embracing me in its depths, taking me captive. I tried to shut the door, but the force of the water was too strong. Soon the whole building was underwater, and I was drowning, a prisoner in this white cage.

I awoke abruptly, regurgitating water. My body convulsing, searching for air as if it had forgotten how to breathe entirely. Accepting oxygen felt foreign to my lungs, and it hit me all at once, making me dizzy and weak. As I opened my eyes, Fifteen was standing over me, his icy palms still clasped to my chest after giving me CPR.

My throat felt scratchy, and raw, as if I had been screaming for hours. My lungs were bruised, and my body stung with an all-consuming itching sensation. Why was I in so much pain? I felt my body, searching for the damage I was sure I'd find.

The people around me were talking to me, but I couldn't make out what they were saying. All I could make out was the unmistakable sound of Ashley's crying.

GAMES OF RUIN

I snapped back into reality, adrenaline giving my body the strength to move. Every bone protested, and every cell cried out in pain, but I ignored them all. I snatched up the Apple beside me and sprinted to Tristan's tank. Jason stopped in front of me, his big sad eyes looking down at me.

"Move," I said, but no words came out, so I tried again. "Move, Jason. We have to get Tristan."

"It's too late Amanda, he's gone." His voice quivered as the tears started to run down his cheeks.

"No, no he can't be... We can still-," I said barging past Jason and climbing up to the top of Tristan's tank.

"Someone help! Why are you just standing there help him!" I screamed, my anger obscuring my voice. Jason and I yanked Tristan from the tank and put his lifeless body on the ground. I immediately started doing CPR, placing my mouth on his, praying that life would seep out of me and into him.

"Come on Tristan, fight." I whispered, "Please, come back to us." My tears began to flow fluently now. Fifteen wrapped his arms around me. "It's time to let him go," he whispered. I wouldn't hear it, I couldn't. I began to press harder into Tristan's chest. "Don't you dare die, Tristan, you promised you'd fight," anger demolished all sadness and took over my soul.

I looked around at everyone's shattered faces, and it only fueled my anger further "What the hell are you guys doing? Help me help him!" I screamed, jerking my body free from Fifteen's clutch.

I continued to do chest compressions, "Tristan, if you can hear me, fight. You have to fight, Fight for your brother, fight for yourself, fight for me. I don't care how or why you do it, Just fight."

"He's gone," Ashley sobbed.

"No, no he's not," I screamed.

The intercom crackled "Blindfolds on, leave the deceased". Fifteen grabbed the bucket of blindfolds, passing them out, each person putting them on as they were handed to them. I was continuing chest compressions when Fifteen made an effort to offer me mine.

"We can't leave him. I won't." I said.

"We have to," he said, trying to reason with me.

"I won't."

He grabbed me and yanked me away from Tristan, my eyes seeing his lifeless body for the last time. I screamed and fought, but it was no use, Fifteen was twice my size and I didn't even have all my strength.

"He has a name," I screamed as I tossed my sanity out the window. "It's not deceased, and it's not number 4, his name is Tristan. You killed him and for what? Amusement? Pleasure? You are sick, and you won't get away with this." My yells went unanswered, no cackle of the intercom, no acknowledgment of my screams.

Fifteen forced the blindfold over my eyes and the next thing I remember was being back in that room with all white walls. But this time it wasn't just a nightmare, it was also my reality.

Chapter Fifteen

Before removing my blindfold, I sensed that the room was dripping with tension, soaking the clothes on my back. I couldn't bring myself to remove the blindfold, as it would mean coming to terms with the fact that he was really gone and that was almost too much to bear.

I didn't want to live in a world without Tristan in it. We hadn't known each other long, but the trauma had bonded us all like a family. We had seen each other at our lowest points and helped each other survive.

I felt a cool hand touch my blistering shoulder and I knew I couldn't pretend any longer. I removed my blindfold, the silky material falling to the ground. We all stood like that in silence for a long time, avoiding eye contact with each other, allowing everyone to grieve in their own way without judgment or condemnation.

Fifteen's hand stayed on my shoulder, keeping me grounded in this reality that I wanted nothing to do with. I slithered away from his comforting hand, the movement attracting an unwanted gaze, making me feel vulnerable and broken.

I was the first to speak, "I can't play a part in this, I won't be a pawn in this twisted game." I spoke more to the camera than anyone in the room.

"We have no choice, Amanda, they'll kill us or worse," Jason said, keeping his voice low.

"They're already torturing and killing us." My voice was getting louder with anger, "If I have to die, I'd rather die fighting to get out of here."

"You can't give up," Haley said in between sobs. "The only thing we have is hope, we can't lose that."

"All of this," I said waving my hands around "is a losing battle, no one here will make it out alive. So why even try?"

"We don't know that." Fifteen whispered, "They could let us go tomorrow, we don't even know why they're doing this or what their plan is"

"Do you really think they're just gonna let us go? We've seen their faces, they plan on killing us. And you're right, I don't know why, some sick version of entertainment would be my guess and I don't know what their plan is, but you're a fool to think we're going to make it out alive." The words tasted bitter on my tongue.

"Why don't you take a minute," Henry said pulling me aside. "The last thing we need right now is to make everyone panic."

He was right, I knew he was. I looked around, only to encounter fear and sadness, my presence only amplifying the sorrow. I needed to distance myself. I couldn't believe this was happening. Straightening up, I went into my room, my red skin aching with every step.

I swung open my bedroom door and stopped dead in my tracks when I saw the one piece of paper that would alter everything I was currently feeling.

GAMES OF RUIN

On my bed sat a picture of my little sister posing with a girl I'd never seen before. The last time I had seen her, she was about half the age she was in the picture, but I'd recognize that face anywhere. The picture was taken in a crowded place, a park maybe? There were several strangers in the background, none of whom I'd recognized.

Wait... is that who I think it is? Tears sliced at my eyes, blurring my vision. I fell to my knees, emotion paralyzing me and I let the tears fall, not caring to mask the sound of my sobs. I cried for Tristan and my sister, I cried for me and this impossible situation I was forced to compete in.

After a while, Fifteen came and embraced me, murmuring comforting words into my hair. It only made the tears fall harder and more frequently. Soon he was crying too, his tears mimicking mine, and we could only sit there like idiots, crying in each others' embrace.

After what felt like years, there were no tears left to fall, and I was left empty. I reached down and grabbed the photo showing it to Fifteen without saying a word.

His face crinkled in confusion, but he studied the photo and put the pieces together faster than I had.

"That's the guy who hunted us, how do you have a picture of him?" Fifteen questioned, not grasping the bigger picture. I inhaled sharply in fear, my breath mingling with terror. Fifteen had just confirmed my worst nightmare.

"His name is James but this girl right here," I said pointing, "is my sister."

"What? I don't understand, how do you have this?" He asked, his brain trying to process.

"You don't get it, Matthew," I said using his real name for the first time. "This isn't just a picture, it's a threat, and it changes everything."

I stormed out of my room and went to his, a picture lay on his bed as well, a pretty blond with perfect teeth, but I wasn't looking at her. I scavenged the background until I found James, that same sick smile on his face. I visited every room and collected all the photos.

Sadness embraced me as I stepped into Tristan's room and found a picture of what looked like an older him, with the same curly brown hair and a smile that could make the world stop spinning. I looked away as the tears threatened to fall once again for a life taken too soon.

I headed back to my room, the photos safely in my pocket only to find Fifteen still staring in shock at my sister or more likely, the unwanted guest lurking in the background. I gestured for him to return it and he complied reluctantly.

"We have to tell the others," I said, and he responded with a simple nod. I whirled around and walked out of the door, the messenger of heartache. Fifteen was heavy on my heels as I reached the others, still as fragile and sad as I'd left them. But this time, I had the puffy eyes to match their own, and we were bonded by the loss of a friend.

Chapter Sixteen

"I have bad news," I whispered, keeping my eyes low. Ashley's sobs grew louder, demanding to be heard. Haley was in the kitchen, making food where tears were the special ingredient. She was keeping busy to distract herself from the pain, but it still had a way of slithering through her best defenses.

Knowing nothing about cooking, Henry still decided to help, desperately needing to be a part of the group. Today he feared the all-consuming feeling of loneliness. Jason had gotten in the shower, the water masking his tears, but the puffy eyes told a tale as old as time.

"I can't handle any more bad news." Haley's tears turned to sobs, making my heart ache.

"Can it wait?" Henry said stepping in front of Haley, trying to protect her from my words.

"It's important," Fifteen said in a whisper.

"I'm sorry, it doesn't matter, it can wait." My eyes fell to the floor. "Let's all just take it easy today and we can talk later. Maybe we could all say a few nice things about Tristan tonight? I think it would help us get some closure." My voice was thick with genuine sorrow.

Ashley nodded, her eyes threatening to swell shut from all the tears. She was not coping well at all, and I felt sad for her.

"But-" Fifteen started.

"That's a good idea, maybe in a few hours?" Henry spoke, knowing the girls needed a little more time for the tears to dry up.

"Sure," I said.

Fifteen shook his head in disapproval, but before he could say anything, I held his hand and directed him toward the bathroom. I turned on the tub, letting the cool water numb my burns.

"We have to tell them," Fifteen said matter-of-factly.

"We can't Fifteen, they won't be able to handle it, not today."

"Why can't they handle seeing a picture of your sister? It doesn't even have anything to do with them." He said, "It's a threat to *you*, to keep *you* in line."

"If I show you something will you promise to keep it between us?" I combed the hair out of my eyes.

"Yeah I guess," he sighed, "but I still think we should tell them, secrets never end well."

"I need you to promise," I pleaded with my eyes.

"Fine, yeah, I promise."

I retrieved the photos from my pocket and presented them to him, one by one. Each time he looked in the background, finding James over and over again. Then I had the last two which I dreaded showing him but I knew I had to get it over with. I handed him the picture that I had found on his bed.

Without hesitation, his features distorted, and his eyes grew dim. His eyes paused for a moment on the main girl, and then he scoured the background, praying it was Jamesless but of course, it was not.

GAMES OF RUIN

He let out a long shaky breath that I didn't know he'd been holding and sat on the bathroom floor, his legs refusing to function.

"What are they going to do to her?" He asked, searching my eyes for an answer that I did not possess.

"Can I ask who she is?" I whispered so low I wasn't even sure he'd heard me.

"She's my girlfriend, we've been together three years".

It was apparent he didn't want to give any more details, so I sat beside him, my hand on his as he processed in silence. Showing him the same compassion he had shown me when the situation was reversed. After a long while I spoke.

"There's one more," I said, handing him the last photo as my tears started to fall again. "It's Tristan's."

He glanced at the photo, his eyes sad as he registered the resemblance "It must be his brother."

I shook my head, trying to shake away the memory of Tristan's lifeless body.

"This changes everything," I said, "we have to play their games, we have to do what we're told, it's not just our lives at stake anymore."

"I know," he said and those two words held an absurd level of understanding, a shared fear that would bond us. A secret desperately needing to be told, but how are you supposed to break a heart that's already been shattered? I couldn't do it, not tonight when feelings were already so raw.

Chapter Seventeen

"Are you okay?" Fifteen asked.
"Not even a little".
"Me neither," he let out a hollow laugh, "but I meant physically, your skin's still really red, and it's blistering in some spots. You were in the tank the longest, you must be in a lot of pain."

"I'm alright," I said, moving my hand from his, suddenly feeling uncomfortable. "My feet hurt the worst, every step is excruciating, but I'll live-" I paused abruptly, realizing how insensitive that last phrase was because not all of us did live. Luckily, he moved the conversation along.

"How's your knife wound healing?"

"It's completely healed, there's not even a scar," I said pulling my pant leg up where the wound should have been.

"How? It was a deep wound, it shouldn't have healed so fast."

"Honestly, I don't know I woke up a couple of days later, and it was just healed. I thought it was weird, but I didn't want to freak anyone out, so I didn't say anything."

"You're superhuman aren't you?" He smirked, brightening the atmosphere.

"I wish, I'd heal all these blisters," I joked, but my smile didn't reach my eyes. "Why aren't you red and blistery? I'm starting to think you're the superhuman." I bumped his shoulder with mine and immediately regretted it as the pain soared through my arm.

"My water wasn't hot, it was freezing cold, I thought I was going to get hypothermia," he said shaking his head. I didn't know which was worse, the hot or the cold. But at that moment, I felt sad for him.

"I'm really sorry they did that to you. I wasn't expecting extreme temperatures, our clue was water, and it was an impossible puzzle to solve. Then, when they explained the rules of the game, they left out the part about freezing and scolding water, and you know they did it on purpose. This whole place is so messed up." I shook my head, "I couldn't open my eyes in the hot water, I knew it would burn and probably make me go blind. Did you know they gave me goggles, so I could watch as I was about to die?"

"I had to take them off you when I did CPR," he said, his eyes sad with the memory. "I don't know what I would have done if you didn't make it." His eyes filled with tears and I found myself comforting him once again.

"It's okay, I'm right here," I said.

"Yeah but you weren't," he slightly shook his head. "You were gone for a long time and there was nothing I could have done to protect you. I'll never feel as helpless as I did in that moment," his voice choked.

"I'm really sorry, you know that right?" I asked.

"For what? Drowning?" he laughed "You never stop surprising me, Amanda."

I ignored his comment. "Thanks by the way," I said.

"For what?" He questioned, and confusion took the place of sorrow.

"For saving my life."

"There isn't a thing in this world that could've stopped me." He walked out the door before I had time to respond.

The group was not ready to talk about Tristan for two more days. I tiptoed around Ashley and Haley as if my simple existence would tear their world in two. Every day we'd sit around the table to eat, even though none of us had an appetite, and every day we'd find ourselves overwhelmed by Tristan's absence.

Three days after Tristan had passed away, it was finally time to say goodbye. We huddled together in a circle in Tristan's room and gave him the best funeral we possibly could.

"I think we should go around and all say something we loved about Tristan," Henry continued when everyone gave their nod of approval. "Tristan was strong, he fought till his very last breath and never showed fear. That was one of the many characteristics I liked about him."

"He was kind when he didn't have to be, he was genuine," Fifteen said.

Jason plopped his head in his hands. "He had his whole life ahead of him, and we will get justice for him. This is not how his story ends," he glared at the camera.

"Forget about the people watching, this is about Tristan," Henry whispered. "What was your favorite thing about him?" He looked at Jason.

"Right, sorry," Jason said. "My favorite thing about Tristan was how thoughtful he was. He always put others before himself."

"He...um," Ashley said, the tears beginning to fall. "He was just incredible," she broke into sobs, unable to finish her thought.

"Shh it's okay Ash, I'll go," I said, my own eyes swelling with tears. "Tristan made me laugh, which is pretty impressive in a place like this," I said with a chuckle, lightening the mood. "And I swear he could've accomplished world peace with that smile of his."

"Let's be honest, he was a stud," Haley said catching us off guard and making us all laugh. "He was my rock through all of this, he stayed with me that first night and helped me find the strength to get up each day. I don't think I would have made it without him."

"His final wish was to tell his brother Lego."

"What?" Fifteen looked at me.

"I don't know what it means, but he said his brother will get it. It's probably an inside joke or something. But if something happens to me, if I don't make it and you guys get out, tell him. It's what Tristan wanted."

"We'll tell him if you can't, I promise," Haley said.

I raised my plastic cup of water, "To Tristan, he's probably up in heaven laughing at this lousy funeral, but he will be missed."

"To Tristan," they all said, clinking their cups with mine, and after that, we all went in to watch Tristan's favorite movie. The mood was still low, but the pain slightly subsided, we had each other to lean on.

I didn't get the nerve to tell them about the photos until the next day. Even then, it wasn't by choice. We had all gathered in the bathroom with the faucet on when Jason told us he had

GAMES OF RUIN

a plan to break out, at that point, me and Fifteen had told them we couldn't, and I had to show them why. One by one, I handed out the photos, and one by one, I watched their hearts break. In turn, it broke my own.

Chapter Eighteen

They took the news as badly as I had expected. I watched as their entire bodies coated in layer after layer of fear. "And how do we know they aren't already dead?" Jason shouted, the sound making me flinch. "James was in each picture, and we know he likes to kill. They're probably already gone." His anger was clouding his judgment.

"They are threatening us, trying to keep us in line, they wouldn't kill their leverage," I said quietly.

"And you," Jason said, directing all his rage at me. "You've known about this for days and didn't think you should tell us? We had a right to know!"

"I'm sorry," I said, not able to look him in the eye "I didn't think it was the right time. We had just watched our friend die." The last few words echoed in the room.

"It's not her fault," Haley said coming to my defense. "I told her I couldn't handle any more bad news. If you want to blame someone, blame me."

"This is stupid guys," Henry said, defusing the situation "We can't turn on each other, we have a bigger enemy and enough to worry about."

"He's right," Fifteen ran his hands through his hair.

"No, you," Ashley shouted looking at Fifteen. "And Amanda don't get to decide what we can and can't handle." Her voice was harsh and raw.

"We wanted to tell you," Fifteen said, "but we had to do what was best for the grou-"

Jason cut him off. "This has nothing to do with you Matthew, you were going to tell us that night, but Amanda decided not to. She's the one who did this, and I bet she's got other secrets she hasn't told us," he finally acknowledged my presence. "I can't believe you would keep this from us after all we've been through together. Explain yourself."

"I said I was sorry," a lump built in my throat, "but I didn't tell you because I didn't want to hurt you. I'm not saying it was the right call, but I'm not the one you're really mad at. You're mad at the people doing all of this, you're mad at the ones who are threatening the people you care about." My voice had risen to a shout. "So if you'll excuse me, I'm not interested in sitting around and being everyone's punching bag. Maybe you should go back to kindergarten and learn how to direct your anger where it belongs but until then, you can leave me the hell alone." I stormed out, suddenly needing to distance myself from everyone.

The fight was stupid, I knew it in the depths of my soul, but it was easier to be angry than it was to be scared, and so I clung to the rage letting it consume me. In the previous days, I had been so terrified that I didn't have the chance to be angry but at this moment, nothing could calm the storm, not even my fear.

I stomped into my room, Haley followed, but she couldn't have picked a worse time to check in on me.

GAMES OF RUIN

"It wasn't fair for them to take their anger out on you. They're just scared." She looked intently at me. "Are you okay?"

"No, you know what I'm not okay. No one here is okay. I'm tired of pretending that everything's fine," my voice came out louder than I intended. "I've had to watch people die and for what? I was hunted by a man with a knife, and barely made it out alive, and look at me." I shouted, waving my arms up and down my body. "I'm freaking pink with blisters coating my body and it hurts. It hurts to walk, it hurts to sit, it hurts to breathe, and I'm just supposed to be okay with it all?"

"You're angry, that's good, it means you care," Haley whispered.

I wasn't done with my rant "Did you know I left a man to die during the hunt?" She shook her head. "He was evil and cruel, but he was a person. He was someone's son, a brother, maybe even a boyfriend and I had to decide to leave him behind and let him die. So yes I'm freaking angry because I should have never been put in a situation where I had to choose to let someone die. I'm angry that these people are threatening my sister and there is nothing in this world I can do to protect her. I'm angry that I was forced into a tank of scorching water. So yeah I'm angry at these people doing this to us, but you want to know the truth?" I asked.

"Yes," sympathy was dancing in her eyes.

"The truth is that as angry as I am with them, I am so much angrier with myself because Tristan is gone. I couldn't hold my breath for long enough, because my body was weak. If I was still conscious when my tank was unlocked, we might have been able to reach Tristan in time. I failed him Haley, and that is something I'll never be able to forgive myself for. So they should be mad at me and so should you." I sighed, blinking back the tears that had filled my eyes. Despite my best efforts, they fell anyway.

"It wasn't your fault you know," Haley said after a few moments.

"Yes, it was, if I could have held on just a little longer he might still be here."

"No Amanda, anyone in your situation would have drowned. We didn't think you'd survive, you were in that tank for so long. You can't possibly blame yourself for drowning," she let out an empty laugh. "Besides if anyone is to blame for Tristan's death, it would be me."

"What?" I asked, her words catching me off guard.

"I slipped and fell, and the key went flying I had to get it and I wasted so much time." She started to cry, "I didn't mean to, I swear I didn't mean to, but I was wet and trying to hurry."

"Shh, it's okay," I said pulling her into a hug, the memory of her falling slammed back into my brain. "It wasn't your fault, they gave us an impossible challenge."

"I killed him, Amanda."

"No you didn't, Tristan wouldn't want you to blame yourself, he loved you, Haley." At that moment, my heart ached for her. I felt responsible for Tristan's death and I wouldn't wish that guilt on my worst enemy let alone this broken girl I held in my arms.

She pulled away and wiped her tears. "I'm sorry, I didn't mean to say all that it just kind of came out."

"You're sorry? I started off yelling at you, then I trauma dumped and started crying." We both burst into laughter.

"You kind of did," she said, and we began laughing again.

GAMES OF RUIN

"But seriously, thank you for listening," I said, "and if you ever need to talk I'm here, plus I kinda owe you one."

"I might take you up on that," she said as she walked out the door.

Chapter Nineteen

The next day, we were taken into the initiation room. Tension was still a little high from the fight, but we had all apologized and made up. Haley and I had bonded and despite all of our differences, we ended up becoming friends. Nonetheless, survivor's guilt lay heavy on our souls.

In the initiation room, we were given our next clue which was the word blindfold. Our video depicted a man, lying in a pool of his own blood, crying out in pain. The tip from someone who had completed level three had come from a handsome blonde man, his words stuck in my head, playing in a loop, giving me goosebumps every time.

"They don't tell you this but if you try to save someone, they will kill you. Three of my friends died on this level because they tried to save a life, don't be a hero, it'll get you killed." After that, the video abruptly ended, it was clear he had more to say, but they didn't allow him to.

The pain in his eyes spoke louder than his voice ever could. His eyes held a story of torment, sorrow, and anger, and it sent a chill down my spine. I feared that after level three, my eyes would tell the same story, that my personality would vanquish and sorrow would become my identity.

After we were led back to our room, we were each given a cup with pills and instructed to take them. We all hesitated, looking at each other, trying to pull together the strength to object.

"W-what are you going to do to us?" Haley stumbled over her words.

"I'm not here to answer questions, I'm just here to make sure you take the pills," the nurse said.

I may be delusional, but I thought I saw a glint of pity in her eyes and there was something in her behavior I hadn't experienced since I was here. She treated us like human beings, not just toys to be played with.

For some reason, I felt like she could be trusted, then again maybe that's what they intended all along and this was just another game. Paranoia attacked my brain, making me question my judgment.

"Please, just tell us what you're going to do, what are the pills? Why do we have to take them?" My words came out more desperate than I intended.

"I can't, you have to take them, it's not up to me. Just take them." The last phrase wasn't a suggestion. Deep down I knew what was at stake if I didn't comply, so I took the pills, despite everything in my body telling me not to. Everyone followed my example, quickly ingesting the pills and displaying their mouths to the nurse.

"Good," she said. "Now I'd recommend you sit or lay down."

We all did, fearing the outcome if we defied and she left the room.

"What did we just take?" Henry was the first to speak.

"I don't know, but I'm guessing it'll knock us out," Fifteen said.

GAMES OF RUIN

"I have to pee, I'll be right back," I said.

"They told us to sit," Jason was agitated.

"I know, but it can't wait," I replied and walked briskly to the bathroom. After I closed the door, I waited a moment, turned on the sink, and shoved my fingers down my throat, making myself vomit. I flushed the toilet, rinsed out my mouth, and returned to the group.

"What if they rape us?" Ashley's voice quivered as she asked, tears filling her eyes.

"They won't do that," I said joining the conversation.

"How do you know?" Haley spoke with tears welling up in her eyes.

"They're disgusting. If they were going to rape us, they'd want us awake and fighting," Fifteen said reading my mind.

"He's right," Henry said, "they wouldn't give us the luxury of knocking us out if they wanted to rape us, they'd just do it."

"Guys, I think you're probably right, but this is a sensitive topic, and you're being really blunt. How about you learn to use a filter?" Jason's agitation progressed to anger.

"Sorry," Fifteen and Henry mumbled

"We were just trying to say that we don't think we've got to worry about that," Fifteen added, feeling uncomfortable.

Ashley nodded, the tears still falling "So then what do you think we need to worry about?"

They continued to discuss our impending demise, but my mind began to wander, and there was no stopping it. The conversation lay on the back burner of my mind as I began to question if I'd regret being awake for whatever they chose to do to me, but it was too late, what's done is done and there's no going back.

Chapter Twenty

My mind spun with possibilities, paranoia urging it on. Was I going to have to pretend to be unconscious as they cut me open? Is that something I could even do? Would they monitor my pulse to make sure it was slow? Was I even going to be able to get away with this?

"Amanda... Amanda, hello?" Henry snapped me out of my thoughts.

"Oh, sorry, what's up?" I said regaining my composure.

"I was just saying that maybe they just gave us a sugar pill, you know to see if we'd actually take it. Maybe they just wanted to see if we'd do as we're told." Henry said, his voice starting to slur.

"Yeah, you're probably right," I said, knowing he wasn't.

"Does anyone else feel-" Haley started.

"Sleepy?" Fifteen finished.

And just like that, their heads fell, all sense of life vanishing from their bodies. I wanted to rush over, to check for a pulse but instead, I did the only thing I could do. Following their lead, I let my head hang and squeezed my eyes shut, wishing my heart would stop pounding.

Anxiety squeezed my breath, holding it captive and then releasing it all at once. One moment, I was hyperventilating and the next It was impossible to exhale. My body had forgotten how to do its most basic function but I had to get a grip.

I attempted to push the panic away, but it refused to leave, so we made a compromise, and it wandered to the back of my mind. I eventually regulated my breathing to a more relaxed rhythm, just in the nick of time. I heard the buzz of the door unlocking and my breath caught in my lungs, refusing to move, but I forced it out slowly.

I heard the sound of wheels rolling across the ground, followed by the commotion of someone lifting someone else onto what I assumed was a stretcher. I heard the wheels skate away and the slam of a door. I wanted so desperately to open my eyes, to understand what was happening.

All I could do was sit and wait, and it was killing me moment by moment. I heard a commotion beside me, someone moving and my frozen body iced over. Did someone else throw up the pill? That couldn't be it because nobody else had gone to the bathroom. I thought the people had all left, but maybe someone stayed back for some reason. My thoughts were going a mile a minute yet nothing made sense.

I concentrated on my inhaling and exhaling and attempted to ease my pounding heart, I stared straight ahead, so that nobody would notice any movement beneath my eyelids. At that moment, time stood still. I was in a room with a potential murderer, defenseless and vulnerable and there was nothing I could do.

After a while, the sound of the wheels returned, and they picked up Fifteen, who was beside me. It took everything in my power to resist recoiling as they accidentally touched my arm. Every time they grabbed somebody and I began to think everyone had left, I would hear movement close by and be reminded I wasn't alone.

Minutes went by, hours maybe before the cart came in to take me. I lay as still as I could and somehow managed to control my breathing despite my climaxing panic. My body lay limp and relaxed, but it was a direct opposition to the state of my mind. Nonetheless, the hands heaving me up, soft but firm did not discover my secret, and I was pushed out the door.

I stayed like that for a long time, way too long, and even though time seemed to blur together, my mind registered that where I was going was a long way away. When I finally came to a stop, I heard the sound of running water, a sink maybe?

The woman beside me spoke for the first time, making my body tense and I prayed with everything I had that they didn't notice.

"She's ready, should I get her undressed?" She asked.

"Yes please, if you don't mind. Then get her hair up and ready for the scan." The voice was rough and raw, without a doubt a man.

Despite my attempts to conceal my fear, I could not slow my breathing. They were going to undress me? Maybe I had been wrong earlier, maybe they were going to take advantage of us. My brain couldn't even begin to think about the scan right now, soon I'd be naked and exposed, I was terrified.

She took my clothes off slowly, stripping me of my dignity in the process. I had to compartmentalize in order to stay still, I had to put what was happening to me at the back of my mind and think of something different.

Unsurprisingly, my mind wandered back to my sister, when we were kids and inseparable. Now I'm not sure if she'd even recognize me if she saw me, besides, she had a new sister now.

My thoughts were dark, just like my soul but even so, anything was better than thinking about the clothes coming off of my body. Fear and sadness now clung to my skin, taking the place of where my clothes should have been. The room was creepily quiet and cold, goosebumps began to sprout on my naked body. Do you get goosebumps when you're sleeping? I prayed the answer was yes as it was beyond my control.

Every fiber of my being was screaming at me, telling me to run, and it took inconceivable strength to disregard the warning. The nurse worked her fingers through my hair, getting it ready to be put up. The man in the room had started to massage something into my skin, it almost felt like lotion, but my nose picked up no scent.

Once the nurse had put my hair up, she placed something on my temples, and a machine beside me started to make a soft humming sound. I focused all my energy on the hum, trying to ignore the fact that the man was getting closer and closer up my thighs.

I had no clue as to what was going on, I found myself wishing I had taken the pill. That I'd be asleep and oblivious, knowledge only brought me pain. Choosing to stay awake wasn't doing me any good, I still didn't know who these people were or what they were doing. There was only one piece of information I found out for sure.

What's happening here is a big operation and my friends and I are at the very center of it.

GAMES OF RUIN

After the man finished putting the lotion on me and the machine stopped humming, they wheeled me off and the next thing I knew, I was alone and in a bed. Even though I'd never thought I'd say this, I prayed I was lying in my bed, in the room with white walls. At least there, I would be sure my friends were close.

I let my body seep into the mattress and I found comfort in its embrace. I wanted to scream, to cry, to find an outlet for my fear. But I had no choice except to lay there, alone with just my thoughts and that was the most dangerous place to be.

I felt disgusting, I desperately needed to get in the shower, to scrub his hands off of me, to wash her out of my hair. I needed to gain my sense of self. This person was no longer me, my free will was stripped away to such an extent that I didn't even know who I was anymore.

I once read that your body produces new skin cells every 7 years, but I prayed to my God above that the article was wrong. I couldn't wait seven years until my skin no longer remembered his hands. My thoughts continued to wander as I forced myself to lie limp.

At this point, neglecting my body's wants and needs had become second nature. I needed to find a way out of this place before it was too late to salvage even an inch of who I used to be.

I remained in that bed for a long while, wishing my mind would go silent, so I could get some rest, but it was hopeless; I was too worked up and terrified. When I finally heard a stir, my bones sharpened beneath my skin as I forced my body to lay still.

There was danger in each moment and I worried that this whole thing wasn't over. But after what felt like an eternity, I heard a voice I'd never forget and every muscle in my body gave way. It was Haley, my Haley, and she was awake and okay.

Chapter Twenty-One

"So let me get this straight," Fifteen said after I filled everyone in on what happened. "They wheeled us off, put lotion on us, and did a scan?"

"Yes... Well, at least that's what they did to me. My eyes were closed, so I don't know if that's what they did to everyone. Plus they wheeled us all off separately" I said and my voice was barely audible above the roaring faucet.

"Are you crazy, if they found out-" Haley started.

"They would've killed you," Ashley squealed.

"Shhh, keep it down," Henry said with wide eyes.

"They didn't find out, I'm fine, they'll never know. I had to know what they were doing to us," I fidgeted with my shirt.

"So we can all assume that the lotion healed our skin right?" Jason whispered.

"Umm... I," I said looking around. I hadn't even noticed, but my pink burnt skin had returned to its usual shade of pale. I scanned the others, seeing no lingering discoloration, and nodded my head.

"It's unlikely our skin would have all healed the same day, so I think it's safe to say the lotion was a healing agent of some sort," Henry said.

"How is that even possible?" Haley asked, shaking her head in shock.

"I don't know, but the same thing happened to me a while back."

"What?" Jason glared.

"I got stabbed in the leg by James's knife, and it healed in a couple of days, I don't even have a scar," I said, my words, not even making sense to my own ears.

"And you d-didn't think to tell us?" Ashley stumbled over her words.

"I thought about telling you, but I didn't want you guys to think I was crazy. We didn't know each other very well back then," I said, holding eye contact with Ashley.

"It's okay, you're telling us now," Henry said.

"Tell us more about the scan, what exactly happened?" Fifteen said, his face mere inches from the roaring faucet.

"They put something on my temples and the machine made a humming noise, that's all I know," I sighed.

"So a brain scan?" Haley asked.

"I think so," I wished I had more information to give them.

"Do you know where they took us?" Jason asked.

"Honestly, I have no idea. But it was far away, like really far. This place must be huge."

"Okay, just one more question," Fifteen's eyes met mine. "Are there any details you haven't told us? Even something small could be important."

"Just one," I said, my eyes displaying hope for the first time, "after everyone fell asleep, they unlocked the doors."

"So?" Ashley said, "they unlock the doors all the time."

"Yes, but they unlocked all the doors and didn't lock them back until after everyone was in bed."

"We have a window," Fifteen said in understanding.

GAMES OF RUIN

"Exactly," I said, somehow feeling lighter.

"But we can't escape guys," Haley said, fear consuming her voice. "If we get caught, they'll kill us, and what about the pictures?"

"They'll hurt the people we care about, I agree with Hales, we can't." Henry whispered.

Dread coated my insides as my mind pictured these people hurting my sister "We can't" I said sounding defeated. Everyone nodded, their eyes as gloomy as mine and I knew the discussion was over.

I walked back to my room, leaving shattered pieces of myself along the way. I had showered multiple times, but his hands remained imprinted on my skin, only visible to my eyes. Choosing to stay awake had taken a greater toll than I liked to admit. The bags under my eyes were just a reminder of that fact.

I lay in bed, letting the embrace of the mattress consume me once again. But this time was different, I felt safer somehow, with my friends awake and alert right outside my door. Right then as my eyes fluttered closed, and my mind began to drift, I heard a knock at my door.

"Hey, it's me. Can I come in?" I'd recognize Fifteen's voice anywhere.

"Mhm," was all I managed to get out, but that was all the invitation he needed.

"Well, hello there, sleepyhead," he said, humor in his voice. I raised my arm and waved at him, my eyes still refusing to open.

"I just wanted to check in, I know things are really awful but I hope you know that I'm here if you ever need to talk about anything." I nodded my head slowly, welcoming the feeling of the blanket on my face.

"Well, I'm going to let you sleep," I could hear the smile in his voice. I shook my head, not wanting to be alone.

"No?" He laughed, "You want me to stay?"

I made a weak nod, the tiredness consuming me and I couldn't fight it anymore. I drifted to sleep, willing the dreams to take me to a better place and they did.

I awoke suddenly and confusion contorted my brain. I was wrapped in another person's embrace, someone's legs were tangled in mine, an arm was thrown over my body. For a moment, I wondered if I was still dreaming.

A slight snore echoed behind me and I felt hot breath on my hair, I wasn't asleep and this wasn't a dream.

All my muscles tightened, and I couldn't bring myself to identify who this stranger was. I didn't want to know the horrors that awaited me or what twisted game this was.

I let out a shallow breath and inhaled the strength I needed to find out what was going on. My eyes traveled down my body, lingering on the arm that didn't belong to me, and I suddenly understood.

This was no stranger at all, it was Fifteen who was lying behind me sleeping. My muscles relaxed and my flight or fight reflexes took a vacation. I felt protected in his arms despite my impending demise in this hell. Suddenly, I felt the need to be closer, to absorb all the good energy my body could possess.

I knew in my very core that trusting people would get you killed but despite my best defenses, Fifteen had managed to seep his way in. His warmth consumed me and I let myself melt in his arms, willing this moment to last.

GAMES OF RUIN

There were so many thoughts going through my mind, but they were quieter somehow. The guilt I possessed that usually felt like it was crushing my soul was lifted, it was still there but lighter like I could finally breathe for the first time.

But like all good things, the moment ended abruptly and without warning as somebody knocked on my door and Fifteen jolted awake. He surveyed the room, panic in his eyes looking for a threat, and he let his body fall back in bed when he found none.

His tired eyes returned, fluttering open and closed, and he gave a sleepish smile as he made eye contact with me.

That one little smile ignited a light within me that I didn't even know existed. At this moment, I knew I was falling for this boy, despite everything telling me not to, despite the circumstances at play and despite the girlfriend he had. I was falling hard, and I prayed to God that he'd be there to catch me when I landed. The knock returned, louder this time.

"Are you awake? We've got food made, and we need to talk about level three" It was Jason's voice.

"Yeah, we'll be right out," I sat up, dragging Fifteen with me. The bad energy returned the moment we left the bed and stepped out the door to face our reality.

Chapter Twenty-Two

After eating a late lunch, we all gathered in the living room to discuss the next level. Nobody wanted to think about it, let alone talk about it, but we didn't have a choice.

"Has anyone figured out what we're going to have to do for level three?" Haley asked.

Everyone shook their heads.

"Come on someone has to have an idea," Jason said already aggravated.

"Well to be fair, we've had a lot going on this week with being drugged and all we haven't had much time to think about it," Ashley said, her voice wavering with emotion.

"I think they give us bad hints on purpose, so we can't figure it out," Henry said.

"He's right," Fifteen said, "the first hint was water and this one is blindfold. Why do they even give us hints at all?"

"Probably to watch us try and solve the impossible, they give us just enough for us to believe we have a chance," Henry said.

"It's all just a big game to them," I shook my head.

"This isn't helping, we need to brainstorm," Jason said, and the room went quiet.

"What do you think? You're the one who's good at this," Haley bumped her shoulder with mine.

"I have a few ideas, but I'm not sure if I should be the one taking the lead. I failed you guys last time." I said, looking at my feet.

Fifteen looked at me. "Hey, you didn't fail us." He lifted my chin and I met his eyes. "Nobody could have known what they were going to do, that's not on you." There was a flutter in my chest, but it was quickly disintegrated by the guilt weighing me down. My skin tingled with an invisible mark left behind as his hand dropped back to his side.

"He's right, it wasn't your fault," Ashley said, withholding eye contact.

"But we will blame you if you don't help us figure out level three," Jason said, he was serious, but everyone laughed at his short temper.

"Okay well, I've been thinking about it and if they're sticking with the theme of games, it could be either hitting a pinata, pin the tail on the donkey, taste test, blind man's buff, or that game where one person is blindfolded, and the other has to direct them through like this obstacle course to get to the other end, I forget the name," I said.

"What's blind man's buff?" Fifteen asked.

"It's like tag but the person who's 'it' is blindfolded and when they tag someone, they have to identify who the person is using just their hands. If they guess right, that person becomes 'it' but if they guess wrong, the person goes free."

"Oh," Fifteen said, "I've never heard of it."

"It all sounds so innocent, but I can't, I can't-" Ashley started, her words becoming sobs.

"We have to compartmentalize," I said, sounding cold. "If we allow ourselves to get emotional, we won't figure this out."

GAMES OF RUIN

Henry shot me a glare, but Jason agreed. "She's right, we can cry later but right now, we need to think rationally."

"I'm sorry Ash," I said, sympathy drowning my words but I continued anyway. "If it's not a game I don't really know, it could be anything. We know there's going to be blood from that video they showed us, maybe that can help narrow it down."

"Yeah, that's a good idea, which of these games could result in bloodshed?" Fifteen asked, running a hand through his hair.

"None of them, I mean they're children's games, they're supposed to be safe, fun even. This is so messed up." Haley's tears had begun to fall ricocheting off the white floor beneath us.

"How can you just sit around and talk about this like everything is fine? We saw a man in a puddle of his own blood, and you want to use that as just another piece to your twisted puzzle?" Henry shouted and it was a sound foreign to our ears, "I'm not going to sit around and be a part of this" He began to stomp off.

"We have to complete level three tomorrow," Fifteen said, his voice soft but firm, "nobody here likes this, but it's something we have to do. If we don't try to figure this out, and we go in there blind, somebody might end up dead. The way I see it, we use every inch of information they'll give us. It's not going to be easy, but we have to think like them to figure this out, and we can't do that if our emotions are in the way." Fifteen sat down and cupped his face in his hands and Henry sat beside him.

"All right, I get it but emotionless doesn't work for all of us" Henry whispered, the sudden decrease in volume tugging my ears. "We are people, you can't just ask us not to feel things."

I looked to Henry, then Ashley and Haley, and the sorrow in my stomach churned. "It helps if you don't imagine it happening to you," I whispered.

"Anyway, if that's out of the way, let's solve this thing," Jason said, moving the conversation along.

Chapter Twenty-Three

We did not, however, end up solving anything at all. After hours of debating the topic, we determined that any game could become violent if you tried hard enough. So we did the only thing we could do at that point, we used the blindfolds in the tub and tried to learn how to function without our sight.

Henry drew a donkey on the whiteboard and we all took turns trying to touch the tail with the marker. We instructed each other in navigating around and over certain objects. We clumsily tried to figure out who each of us was using only our hands, and we attempted to guess different smells and foods. Despite our best attempts to utilize what we had, we all still found ourselves struggling.

By the end of the night, our accuracy, listening skills, and other senses had improved with the practice. However, we were nowhere near perfect and that fact haunted us. We were trying to practice so many different skills and we were stretched too thin, our odds were not looking very good.

"I think we've practiced enough," Haley said, taking a seat.

"No, we need to keep going," Jason shook his head.

"Haley's right, we should try to get some rest, we don't need everyone sleep-deprived tomorrow," I shrugged.

"Yeah, I agree. Not to mention the fact that we might not even be practicing for the right thing," Fifteen said, agitated.

"Yeah, I'm exhausted," Henry began to stretch.

"Well, I guess I'm going to head to bed," Fifteen said walking away.

"Goodnight guys," Henry was already at his door.

"Night," we said in unison. Jason and Ashley followed leaving just me and Haley in the living room.

"You staying up?" I asked.

"Yeah, a little while longer, I don't think I'd be able to sleep anyway," she said.

"Yeah me either," I tugged at the blanket and turned the TV on.

We sat like that, for a long time, in silence watching the TV. My thoughts grew louder with each passing second but knowing I wasn't alone comforted my soul. I thought about Fifteen and how I had woken up beside him and we had pretended like nothing ever happened but every time I saw him, he took a little bit of darkness and replaced it with light.

He's the boy that gives me butterflies and makes me feel alive. I'm so terrified of losing him, but then again, he's not even mine. The only place I've ever even felt somewhat beautiful was in the reflection of his eyes. Even still, I have a feeling I'll break my own heart loving him.

My warm and fuzzy feelings were soon brought to an abrupt end as my mind drifted to tomorrow, a day that might end up being my last. Terror danced in my chest, as my mind replayed the video of the man screaming, surrounded by dark red venom from his body. Haley dragged me from my thoughts and I flinched at the sound of her voice.

GAMES OF RUIN

"Do you think we're going to live?" Haley asked and I instantly knew she was having the same dark thoughts I was.

"Honestly?" I asked and she nodded, her eyes full of sadness, "I don't know." My heart ached at the thought of losing her. These people had become my family, I loved each and every one of them not just despite their flaws but rather because of them. Losing any one of them would break my heart in two.

With that being said, my world would absolutely tilt upside down if I were to lose Haley or Fifteen. They are my people and my life wouldn't be the same without them.

"I'm so scared, Amanda," Haley sobbed.

"Me too," I whispered in her hair as I pulled her into my arms.

"Why do you think they're doing this?"

"I don't know, I used to think they were doing it just because they could. I thought It was a big game to them and they did it as a sick form of entertainment."

"And now?"

"Now I think there's something bigger going on. I don't know what or why but I'm going to figure it out." I said, getting angry at the thought.

"How?" She asked.

"I don't know yet," I admitted, "but I think this is the clinical trial, I just think they omitted the important things in the brochure."

"Like the fact that they planned to capture and torture us?" It wasn't really a question.

"Yeah, something like that."

"And what about level three?" She asked, "I don't know how much more I can take."

"We'll get through it together," I whispered with sad eyes.

"Me and you stick together no matter what?" She asked between sobs and I nodded as my own tears threatened to fall.

"I need you to promise," she said.

"I promise you, Haley," I whispered.

Chapter Twenty-Four

I opened my eyes in a panic, my feet hit the floor and my hands instinctively raised to meet the danger.

"Easy there tiger," Fifteen said, gently grabbing my arms and putting them at my side. "I'm not trying to fight you," he laughed.

My brain recorded the sound and filed it in the favorites folder of my mind. His hands lingered on my skin, captivating my breath and as soon as he let go, my skin ached with his absence. I looked up to see his eyes, filled with fear and sadness, and it broke something inside of me.

For a moment, just a quick few seconds I had forgotten that today was the day my life would be turned upside down again. That the floor beneath me would crumble again. That my shattered heart would break again.

I was unsure of a lot, but I did know one thing for certain, level three would destroy me and I didn't know if I'd ever be able to recover.

We ate breakfast in silence, each and every person withholding eye contact. It was a funeral, and we didn't know which one of us would end up dead. As I met Jason's gaze, his eyes were lit with a flame even more intense than usual. He was always angry, but it was only because he cared, he was just a wounded soul who expressed himself in the wrong way. He was just a boy, misunderstood and hurting, and I couldn't imagine losing him, not today, not ever.

Then, my eyes meandered to Henry; he was protective and gentle despite all odds. He stood up for what he believed in, and he was always there to comfort someone in need. He was selfless that way and I wondered if someone had ever reciprocated that comfort.

I hoped they had because he was in just as much pain as the rest of us. Although Henry and I hadn't had a chance to become close, he was still a part of me, they all were.

Ashley was whom I looked at next, her puffy eyes were raw as per usual. Ashley felt things at an all-consuming intensity which in the real world might be a good thing, but here it was a recipe for destruction. She was the one I felt the worst for, the one I wanted to protect at all costs because I didn't think she could handle much more pain.

I looked to Fifteen and Haley, each holding a half of my heart. No force in the known universe could ever disconnect me from these two. Fifteen made me feel at home in this prison and that alone defied all sense of rationality. He made me feel things I had never felt before, and he had the ability to erase my pain, even just for a moment, it was a priceless quality in a place like this.

Haley had become my best friend, she understood me in a way nobody else had. She could tell when I needed comfort and when I needed space, and she didn't hesitate to put me in line if I went too far. She was soft and vulnerable, and she was good for me, she dulled my cold and distant personality. If I lost either one of them, I don't think I'd be able to continue living this life.

GAMES OF RUIN

Tears were threatening to fall, and I looked away, refusing to think of this as the last time I'd see them alive. Instead, I thought about myself and the possibility of it being my last day, that was so much easier. Self-hatred had become such a part of me that I welcomed the idea. My guilt for those I'd left to die pushed me to believe I deserved to die too, and the sooner, the better.

"I feel like we should do something, we need a distraction," Henry said, breaking the silence.

"You want to play a game right now?" Jason asked, agitated.

"It's better than sitting here with our thoughts," Henry began fidgeting with his shirt.

"Two truths and a lie?" Fifteen suggested.

"Sure, you can go first since it was your idea," Henry said.

"Okay um," Fifteen started, "I dropped out of high school. I have a dog named Bo, and I was a foster kid."

"The dog I believe," Henry said his voice still sad.

"You don't really seem like the dropout type," Haley whispered more to herself than anyone.

"So foster kid is the lie?" Jason asked, still hesitant.

"Nope," Fifteen said, "I don't have a dog."

"Why'd you drop out?" I asked.

"School just wasn't my thing, I had to work full time to support myself and I just couldn't juggle both," he immediately looked at his feet.

"I'm sorry," I whispered putting my hand on his. "It isn't fair that you had to grow up so fast."

"It's okay, it is what it is. Your turn," he said nodding his head at me.

"Let me think," I said, then after a moment I continued, "I wanted to become a criminal psychologist."

Jason interrupted, "wanted? Like past tense?"

"Yeah I mean, I don't think I'm going to make it out of here alive so past tense."

"You can't think like that," Haley said, "we'll make it, we have to."

I ignored the positivity, "Okay, I *want* to become a criminal psychologist better?" She nodded, and I continued, "I've never been in love and my favorite movie is Jaws."

"I don't even know what a criminal psychologist does, but you're smart so that ones probably true," Henry said.

"Yeah, you made it too easy, you've never been in love is the lie," Jason said.

Everyone agreed, nodding their heads in approval. "You guys suck at this," I said, a smile tugging at my lips.

"You're joking," Fifteen said searching my eyes.

"Nope, Shrek's my favorite movie, not Jaws," I said.

"You've never been in love?" Ashley whispered, her voice full of doubt.

"Why's that so hard to believe?" I asked, "I'm only 17"

"Well because..." Jason started. "We might be about to die, so I'm just going to say it."

"What?" I asked as confusion tugged my brows together.

"You're hot, like really hot," Jason said and everyone started laughing.

"Whatever," I laughed and I hoped they wouldn't notice my face getting red. I never truly saw myself as beautiful, I have boring straight, light brown hair that falls a little past my shoulders. My face has soft curves and my eyes are a dull hazel color. I never liked the girl in the mirror, truth be told, I'm nothing special.

"You really are," Henry's words pulled me from my thoughts. I looked up to meet his eyes when Fifteen's cough drew my attention and I looked over. His jaw was set, eyes cold, it was a side of him I hadn't seen before. He was staring right at Jason and Henry and if looks could kill, they would have died a thousand deaths.

Either Fifteen had a vendetta with these two, or he was a taken man, jealous for a girl that wasn't his. Either way, I needed to push the conversation along, and I needed to do it now.

"I think it's Haley's turn-" The crackle of the intercom interrupted my sentence and fear pumped through my veins. Nobody in the room breathed, we could no longer pretend things were fine, level three was here. The tension in the room soaked the clothes on my back.

"Blindfolds on," it spat. Fear held us captive for a moment, none of us daring to move, then suddenly, we all rushed into action, looking for the blindfold bin.

"I see it," I said moving towards the bin, it had been in front of our faces the whole time, but we were blinded by fear.

Chapter Twenty-Five

Once everyone had their blindfolds, we gave each other one last look before pulling them down. I heard Ashley's sobs grow louder, but the rest of the room was silent. My mind however was the opposite, screaming at me to run, telling me danger was near. It was a sound I'd have to ignore because what my mind didn't know was that running would result in sudden death.

I felt Fifteen's hand interlock with mine and I gave it a squeeze of gratitude. I didn't know if he did it for his comfort or mine but either way, it was nice to know I wasn't alone.

Just then, when my mind finally quieted a little, the door buzzed open and all sense of rationality left me. I began to hyperventilate, the air going in and out of my body at impossible speeds.

I had to get it together, they would see my fear and find a way to use it against me, so I needed to at least pretend like I was fine. I jumped bodies from Amanda to number three where strength was waiting, strength I didn't even know I had.

"Don't forget, our clue is don't be a hero. Whatever happens, we can't help each other, or we die." I said with tears filling my eyes. The silence stung my ears and my pulse picked up its pace, "I need to hear you say that you heard me."

"We heard you," I held on to their voices, not wanting to focus on anything else.

"I've never been much of the hero type anyway," Jason laughed but I could hear the terror in his voice.

"No more talking," It was a voice I didn't recognize, probably our escort. The voice held authority and we didn't say another word.

They handcuffed us to the bar, with more force than usual, and led us out of our room, I focused on the turns we took, adding the directions to the map in my mind. If I chose to focus on anything else, my mind would self-destruct with fear. So I repeated the route, over and over in my head, pushing all other thoughts aside.

When we got to the room and were instructed to remove our blindfolds, my eyes instantly met James's. My blood iced over, and my breath halted, flashbacks from the hunt haunted my soul. I was feeling so many emotions: Anger, Disgust, Hatred, Fear, Sadness, but they all blurred together to create one simple emotion.

Rage.

Sanity had left, leaving no trace that it was ever truly there. I lunged at James, fists balled, despite that large hunting knife he had by his side that had already stolen so many lives. He drew his knife as I got closer and the amusement dancing in his eyes only made me angrier.

Fifteen grabbed me, pulling me back to him with such force, that my body slammed into his. I kicked and fought, trying to get free of his grasp, but he was too strong.

"You're sick you know that?" I screamed holding James's eyes captive.

GAMES OF RUIN

"I need you to stop, you're going to get yourself hurt," Fifteen whispered in my ear, but I ignored him.

"What is so wrong with you that you have no regard for human life?" I challenged.

Silence pierced through the room. "So, you don't fraternize with your victims is that it?" I looked at him with a hate so strong that it made my body tremble.

Fifteen spun me around and pushed me up against the nearest wall in one swift motion. He lifted my chin, so my eyes collided with his, and it was the first time that I dropped eye contact with James.

"I told you to stop." His voice was low but stern and that coldness I had seen in his eyes earlier had returned. He was rough and raw and I could see a glimmer of his own rage staring back at me.

I looked at James one last time, "I'd tell you to go to hell, but you'd probably enjoy it there." After catching a glimpse of that sick smile, I turned my back, needing to look at anything else.

James clapped his hands together, making every bone in my body jump "Now that the show's over, let's get on with the game." He said cheerfully. The sound made me nauseous.

"Today, we'll be playing pin the tail on the donkey but with a twist," he paused.

My eyes met Haley's and she sent me a silent thank you. It was a game we had practiced. Hope ignited within me, maybe we do have a fighting chance.

"The rules are as follows: One person will be strapped down, so they can't move as another is playing the game. The person playing the game must place the tail on the donkey perfectly to win. If they don't, the person strapped down gets punished. These two wheels will be spun to determine what the punishment will be."

He withdrew the curtain covering the wheels. One of the wheels had body parts listed which were as follows: Arm, Leg, Face, Ear, Foot, and Hand. The other wheel had action words: amputate, stab, slice, punch, taze, and inject. I take back what I previously thought, we don't have a fighting chance.

"This process will be repeated until the tail is placed perfectly on the donkey, and then the two will switch places."

"Your groups will be," he said as he drew two pieces of paper from a bowl, "Haley with Henry," there was a brief pause as he grabbed two more. "Amanda with Matthew and Ashley with Jason."

Silence hung in the air for what felt like forever.

"Any questions?" He asked. We all shook our heads dumbfounded. But what was there to say?

"Great, you have two minutes to talk with your partner, you can come up with a game plan and figure out who will go first. The clock starts now," James said.

I was already standing beside Fifteen, but I turned and faced him.

"Do you want to go first or do you want me to?" I asked. My mind was still processing what I had just heard and what we were about to have to do.

"I don't know, I guess I'll go first," He said and I just nodded my head. Words had begun to fail me, I couldn't think of one thing I could say to make this situation okay.

GAMES OF RUIN

"I won't let anything happen to you, okay?" He said, tucking a strand of hair behind my ear and my heart caught in my throat.

"You can't promise me that, it's mostly up to luck with those stupid wheels," I said.

"We'll just have to do our best, but we practiced last night. I think it'll be okay," he said, and I turned my head, so he wouldn't see me cry.

"Hey look at me," he said cupping my face with his hands. "We're going to make it past this level, you and me against the world right?"

"Yeah," I said wiping my tears, "I just never imagined our world would be so scary and sad. We don't even have a fighting chance."

"We do though, together we do," He said and every muscle in my body told me to believe it, to trust him, but it just wasn't that simple.

Chapter Twenty-Six

The timer buzzed, and the sound made me flinch, we were out of time. I looked around the room until I made eye contact with Haley. Her fear was contagious, and I said a silent prayer that God would keep her safe. She was paired with Henry, so her life was in his hands now and I feared the worst.

"All right, who's getting strapped down first?" James asked.

"Umm," Haley said, and her voice was small, "I am".

I watched in horror as she walked over to the bed, and he strapped her down like she was no longer a person but an animal. I felt sad, he was going to hurt Haley, my Haley, and he was going to enjoy doing it.

I looked at Fifteen, not wanting to watch any longer. His jaw was tensed and by the fire in his eyes, I could tell he hated seeing this as much as I did.

I placed my hand in his, to comfort myself more than him, but I saw his muscles relax a little. By now, Henry had put the blindfold on and had spun around in a circle three times. He was then placed in front of the donkey and my breath stalled in my lungs as he just barely missed the Velcro strip where the tail is supposed to go.

"Did I get it?" His words trembled as he spoke.

"No," James said with a smile.

Henry took off his blindfold, disappointed with himself. Then he spun the wheels, it landed on the words inject and face. James walked to a table and grabbed a syringe containing a yellow liquid.

"I'm so sorry, Haley," I could hear the shame in Henry's voice.

"It's okay, it'll be fine," she replied.

"What are you going to inject her with?" I asked, my fear hidden behind a facade of anger.

"Wouldn't you like to know," James smirked as he stuck the needle in her cheek, only pulling it out when the syringe was empty. It took unimaginable strength for me to keep my feet planted, more than anything, I wanted to help her.

To my surprise, Henry was successful on the next round and my whole body relaxed as James undid the straps on Haley's body. However, the relief did not last long.

"I don't feel right," Haley said standing up.

"What do you mean, are you okay?" I asked, my voice trembling with desperation.

"I don't know, I feel... I feel kind of weird. I don't know if I can do this," her words slurred together.

"You have no choice," James spoke with a threatening authority.

"You can do it, Haley," I said, what else was there left to say?

She pulled her blindfold down and my whole body tensed as I saw James touch her to spin her around. She stumbled over to the board and placed the tail on the donkey's head.

She ripped the blindfold off and stumbled over to the wheels, now completely disorientated by the mystery liquid.

GAMES OF RUIN

The wheels landed on taze leg. I heard the sound of the taser and Henry screamed out in agony.

Only seconds later, James instructed Haley it was time for round two, and she stumbled back to the board, her steps seeming harder and harder to take. I was filled with dread as I saw her nearly, but not quite, place the tail in the right spot.

She glanced at Henry, her eyes glistening with tears, and spun the wheel which yielded the words punch and arm.

James beamed at Henry as he reared back and struck his forearm.

Henry cried out in pain and my body shivered at the sound. "It feels broken, is it broken?" Henry yelled, struggling against the bonds, terror dripping from each syllable.

I looked closer, seeing a lump in his forearm that hadn't been there before, "no, it's not broken, you're okay" I lied and I was surprised by the calm in my voice.

"Are you sure? It really hurts," he said, closing his eyes.

"Yeah, we're sure," Jason said. "You're going to be okay," his voice was shaky but firm.

"Don't lie to the man," James laughed. "Of course, it's broken."

"Oh, so you torture and kill but lying's where you draw the line?" I glared and my eyes said more than my mouth ever could but he didn't respond.

I looked at Haley "You can do this Haley, you have to do this. I don't know what you were injected with, but you have to fight it, remember what we practiced?"

She nodded her head in understanding, but I wasn't sure she understood at all.

The breath caught in my lungs as I watched her trip her way to the board and just barely miss the Velcro.

"That has to count," I pleaded, fearing for the worst.

"She's drugged," Ashley sobbed. "That has to be close enough right?"

Without saying a word, James just signaled for Haley to go to the wheel, and I felt a heavy sensation in my chest. She spun the wheel, but it was evident, that her mind was in a different universe. Henry was doomed because Haley was drugged, this game was the opposition of fair.

When the wheels stopped spinning, they landed on slice leg and James was happy to accommodate. He grabbed the scalpel from the table and worked his way over to Henry.

"I can't watch this," Ashley said as she continued to sob.

"It's okay Haley, it's not your fault," Henry said, refusing to look at James.

"You don't have to do this, it isn't fair," I said.

"How can you drug her and still expect her to be able to do this?" Jason shouted, rushing forward as James started to slice Henry's leg. I felt Henry's scream in the bottom of my soul and tears pooled in my eyes.

I watched as Fifteen grabbed hold of Jason and pulled him back, refusing to loosen his grip.

"Don't be a hero," were the only words Fifteen said, his voice was raucous, and I heard it even over the screams. When I got the nerve to look back at Henry, there was a big gash in his lower thigh, blood had begun to drip on the floors, every drop ricocheting his pain.

The screams had stopped, but his face spoke of immense suffering and I longed to be anywhere but here. I looked at

GAMES OF RUIN

Haley, she was staring at a corner like it held the answer to all our prayers, but there was nothing there.

"Hey," I whispered, then louder, "Haley look at me" An entire lifetime passed before her eyes met mine. I ignored the vibes of pain evaporating from Henry's body and I disregarded the sound of Fifteen holding Jason back. "You have to get it this time," I said. "Haley, do you hear me? I need you to hear me. If you don't get it right this time, Henry will bleed to death and die. Please, Haley, Please hear me." Tears rolled down my face as I spoke.

James walked over to spin Haley in circles before she had the opportunity to reply. She walked closer to the board, and the air in the room became charged with tension.

We all knew that the fate of Henry lay in her hands, and we were terrified she'd drop it. When they gave Haley the drug, Henry was handed a sentence of torture and death, and we were unable to intervene. All we could do was sit back and watch. It was as much our torment as it was his.

Haley took step after stumbled step, and each one felt like a stab to my chest. Slowly she raised her hand and placed the tail, by some miracle from God, she placed it on the Velcro strip.

"She did it, Henry she did it, you're going to be okay" Ashley squealed. I heard Henry sigh in relief as James set him free.

Chapter Twenty-Seven

With a limp, Henry made his way to us and immediately removed his shirt and tied it around his wound.

I wanted so desperately to run to him, to help. "You have to tie it tighter," I said and he pulled it as tight as he could with his one good arm, wincing in pain. Everything in my body told me to help him but there was nothing I could do without putting my own life in jeopardy. So I stayed with stagnant feet and let the light inside me die little by little as I pondered how worthless my existence was and how there was nothing I could do to help my friends.

"Who's next?" James's eyes were lighter now, for him psychotic tendencies went hand in hand with happiness.

Fifteen didn't give James the luxury of a verbal answer. Instead, he climbed onto the bed and stared at the ceiling as James strapped him down.

James then headed towards me and with every step he took, I had to talk myself out of running. I put the blindfold on, not wanting to see his face. I had to keep my attention on the task, as Fifteen's life hung in the balance. James's touch sent a shudder through me, his hands felt like fire against my exposed skin, and fear raced through me.

I tried to pretend that these hands belonged to someone else, anyone else but my mind was stubborn and refused to do so.

When he had finished spinning me and released his grip, I could finally breathe again and my body strived to erase the sensation of his embrace. I walked forward, taking my steps slowly and with calculation. Hurting Fifteen was the last thing in this entire world I wanted to do so I needed to get this right. I raised my hand and placed the tale.

"Did I get it?" I asked, the calmness in my voice gone now. Dread coated my insides and I knew the answer before anyone got the chance to reply.

"No," Jason said, and that one word destroyed my world. I ripped the blindfold off and walked over to the wheels. My eyes stayed pinned to the ground, my shame kept me from looking at Fifteen in the eye.

I spun the wheels which resulted in Fifteen getting punched in the face. The only noise he made was a small grunt and I finally got the nerve to look at him.

"I'm sorry," was all I could say as tears fell from my eyes. No words could express how much it hurt me to see him in pain.

"It's okay, it could have been worse, I'm okay. You can do this." He said and up until that point, I had somehow forgotten I'd have to do this again.

I looked at James for the first time "Why, why are you doing this?" I shook my head, willing this whole day to be over.

"Put the blindfold on Three," He said, using my number instead of my name and he sounded aggravated.

"So we're not even people to you? Is that how you justify it?" My voice rose to a shout.

GAMES OF RUIN

"I won't tell you again," he took a step toward me and I pulled the blindfold over my eyes because ultimately, he held all the power.

My entire body tensed up as he spun me around. How ironic, I wasn't such a tough guy after all. With shaky hands, I placed the tale once again. This time, I didn't ask the group, instead I ripped off the blindfold needing to see for myself. I prayed my eyes were malfunctioning, but of course, they were not.

The walk of shame to the wheels felt longer somehow like time had stopped. My arms reached out and spun the first wheel without my mind even telling them to do so.

My body was not my own, I was no longer in control. The wheel stopped spinning at the word ear and before I was able to spin the second, Fifteen spoke.

"It's okay Amanda," he said.

I snapped back, "No, it's not, none of this is okay. If I kill you, I won't be able to live with myself, can't you understand that? I don't want to be in a world that doesn't have you in it. So it's not okay and I don't need you or anyone else to lie and tell me it is." My eyes flicked to the rest of the group, they were all staring at me with sympathy. Now I was the broken one in need of comfort and I hated every second of it.

"Spin the second wheel," James bellowed and my body quaked at the sound. My arms reached up and spun the second wheel, obeying his orders. It landed on inject and my body relaxed a little.

"For what it's worth, I care about you too," Fifteen said with a laugh, mocking my previous outburst. "But if you don't get it this time, I'm going to sue you when we get out of here."

My eyes would have rolled if the stakes weren't so high but my mind couldn't process funny right now, pain was all I knew. I watched as James grabbed a syringe, this one held a clear liquid, possessing a new form of horrors. I prayed to my God above that it wasn't fatal and looked away as he injected it into Fifteen's ear.

I looked at the board, studying every inch of the donkey, memorizing even the smallest details. I focused so hard, that I hadn't even heard James come up behind me. He placed his hands on my shoulders and out of instinct, my body jerked away, hard. He let out a small laugh as he soaked in my fear. I put the blindfold on and spun around, desperate for him to let me go.

When he finally did, it was too late, his touch was already ingrained in my skin, an invisible scar. I took step after step, putting Fifteen out of my mind, replacing him with denial which I clung to like my life depended on it.

At that moment, I wasn't in this place, my friends weren't in danger, nothing was real. I was playing a children's game, and I wanted to win, that's all I told myself.

Chapter Twenty-Eight

My breath started a steady rhythm and my hands stopped their tremble. A calm washed over me and I soaked it in. I reached out my hand and placed the tale with a confidence I didn't know I had.

"You did it," Ashley said, voicing what I already knew in my mind to be true. I held back tears of relief as I pulled off my blindfold and entered back into this tragic reality.

The next thing I knew, I was in that bed, getting strapped down, and I did my best to delay the panic that was clenching my chest. James slid a finger down my face and leaned down to whisper in my ear. "I've got a special surprise for you." I wriggled in my straps, distorting my body to get free, but it was no use. Panic had won the battle against rationality. I was vulnerable and afraid and James loved every moment of it.

"I'm not going to do anything to her, you can calm down," James chuckled.

Confusion pricked my brain until I spotted Jason trying to hold Fifteen back. The fire in his eyes could incinerate anything in its path and I knew I had to say something before he did something stupid. "It's okay Fifteen, just play the game, so I can get out of here," I said, trying to mask my fear.

He regained his composure and Jason let him go. I couldn't see Fifteen as he placed the tail but the outcome hardly mattered. No amount of physical pain could compare to the torment of watching someone get hurt because of me, so the worst part was already over.

I heard the sound of the wheels spinning and prepared myself for the pain I was undoubtedly going to experience. James stood over me, with a scalpel, "I'm going to enjoy this." He whispered in a voice so low, that only I could hear it.

"Don't be a hero," I yelled, reminding the group, pleading with Fifteen to stay sane. Then I bit my tongue as James sliced a line from my ear to my lips. A whimper was all I allowed to come out of my mouth.

My face throbbed, sending me a constant rhythm of pain. The blood began to trickle down my face, but there was only one thing I could focus on.

James's words played on a loop in my mind, he said he had a surprise for me. My mind tried to process, to try to understand what he meant. Either something truly awful was coming or he was trying to scare me. Either way, I wanted no part of it. I struggled under the straps, praying that this wasn't real, that it was all just a cruel nightmare, that any moment I'd wake up.

The pain shooting through my body served to tell me that I was wrong, that this was real and the straps reminded me that there was no escape. Ashley's voice broke me from my thoughts.

"He did it," was all she said and James came over to undo my straps. I hadn't even realized Fifteen had started round two, I guess my thoughts engulfed me so entirely that I missed it. He undid the last strap and I got up, touching my wrists as if my arms did not believe they were truly free.

GAMES OF RUIN

My eyes collided with Fifteen's, it was a clash of fire and Ice, and my soul melted a little with every passing second.

"Are you okay?" I asked, and the whole world fell away as he wrapped his arms around me as if he was trying to shield me from this cruel reality.

"I am now," he said, and I pulled away to look at the bruise forming around his eye.

"Do you feel okay?" I asked.

He nodded, understanding what I meant "Yeah, I think the liquid he injected me with was just a numbing agent, I feel fine".

My attention was drawn to Jason as he walked to the board and managed to place the tail perfectly with his first attempt.

"He did it, Ash," I said, relief pooling in my stomach.

Her sobs grew louder, but I knew, they were tears of relief, not fear or sadness.

"What a waste of my time," James mumbled as he undid her straps and then proceeded to strap Jason down.

My gaze shifted to Haley, who was sitting on the ground with her eyes shut.

"Haley," I whispered, but she didn't move and instinctively, I feared for the worst.

"Haley," I said louder, more desperate this time. Her eyes jolted open as if she had been sleeping. My muscles relaxed a little after seeing proof of her continued existence.

"Are you alright?" I asked, knowing she wasn't. Her eyes wandered, and she shrugged, and I knew it was the only answer I was going to get. Her eyes were cloudy and glossed over, she was so incredibly high, but I knew there was nothing I could do for her right now.

Chapter Twenty-Nine

The noise of the wheel spinning caught my attention, it was a sound I had grown to despise. I held my breath until both wheels had been spun, and then I exhaled with relief. It landed on the words stab and ear, Jason would survive.

James grabbed a small knife and plunged it through Jason's earlobe, splitting it in two. To my surprise, Jason didn't make a sound.

"Weird time to get my ears pierced but hey I'll take it," Jason said, making me smile a bittersweet smile. Ashley laughed through tears, but the moment didn't last long as she was soon blindfolded and playing round two.

A horrified gasp filled the room as Ashley missed the velcro strip again and the wheels landed on inject foot.

James seized a syringe full of a transparent liquid and inserted it into Jason's foot.

"I'm sorry Jason, I'm trying my best," Ashley sobbed.

"It's okay Ashley," he said, "It's not your fault."

A few moments later as Ashley began round three, Jason began to panic.

"Guys, I can't feel my foot, something's wrong." Ashley placed the tail, missing yet again.

"I think it's a numbing agent, you'll be okay," Fifteen said with a surprising gentleness.

"I don't want to, I can't do this," Ashley said as James motioned her to the wheels. "I'm sorry Jason, I'm really sorry," her sobs became louder.

"You have to Ash," Jason said "I'll be okay, just spin the wheels," his voice was soft.

"Or don't and see what happens," James threatened.

Without requiring any more encouragement, Ashley spun the first wheel, and it stopped at foot, then with a deep breath she spun the second wheel, and it ended on slice.

James grabbed the scalpel once again and made a clean cut along the length of Jason's foot, I winced as I watched, but Jason didn't make a sound.

"Can we get this over with already?" Jason asked with a nervous voice.

"He already did it," I said confused, then I realized "Oh, the numbing agent, you probably just couldn't feel it"

"Lucky me, I guess it worked out," Jason laughed, but it was void of humor.

I looked over at Henry as Ashley prepared to play another round. His shirt was completely saturated with blood and his complexion was getting paler and paler with every passing moment.

"Hold on Henry, you just have to hold on, we're almost done. You're going to be okay," I whispered.

"I don't know what you mean, I'm just peachy," he said with a weak laugh that made my heart hurt.

I looked back at Ashley just in time to see her place the tail perfectly. A sigh of relief washed over me as Jason was taken out of the straps. The level was over and we somehow all made it out alive.

GAMES OF RUIN

Henry and Haley could barely walk, Jason hopped on one leg because his other leg was refusing to function and Fifteens' eye had turned an awful shade of blue. But we were all still here and that's what's important.

I approached Haley and covered her eyes with a blindfold, as I knew she couldn't do it by herself. I was in the process of putting my own on when I heard James speak.

"Did I say we were done here?" He asked, and my body froze over with terror.

"We did what we were told, just let us go," Jason said.

"That's the thing," he said with a pause. "One of you did not do as you were told, and I was permitted to punish you as I see fit." He stared into my soul and I willed myself to be smaller, to escape his gaze.

"We all participated," Fifteen said, stepping in front of me. I racked my brain, trying to figure out what I had done wrong. How had I not listened? I did everything I was supposed to didn't I? His glare made me second-guess everything I knew to be true. At the end of the day, it was my fault, it was always my fault.

"Yes, you all did very well," he said.

"I'm sorry," I stammered, "for whatever I did, I'm sorry."

"Sorry doesn't make up for throwing up the pills," he took a step towards me. "You blatantly disobeyed an order."

My hands began to tremble, and my face turned an ungodly shade of red. I felt all eyes on me, but how had he known? I had no time to think, I had been caught and there was nothing I could do to get out of this mess.

"At a loss for words?" He smirked, and I just stared, dumbfounded. "I'm going to make this easy for you, I'll let you choose who I kill."

"N-No, please," I cried.

"Choose," he said pulling out his knife, "and don't get any bright ideas, if you try anything, you'll all be dead by the end of the day." He paused to look at Fifteen. "Even if you managed to kill me, there are dozens of others to exact my revenge," his tone made me shiver.

My mind spun. "Kill me," I whispered, it was my immediate answer. I hadn't even given myself time to think. Then I spoke louder, confident in my answer. "I'm the one who did it, don't hurt them. I choose me. Kill me." A solitary tear trickled down my face.

"As tempting as that sounds, I'm going to say no," James smiled.

"W-what do you mean? You said I could choose," I stumbled over my words with a sob in the bottom of my throat, and I shoved it down.

"Choose one of your friends, or I kill her. You have three seconds," In one swift motion, he grabbed Haley and held the knife to her throat. Having her life a stake sobered her up a little. "You don't have to do this," Haley cried.

"Three," he said.

My vision blurred, and my life came crumbling down before my very eyes.

"Two."

My breath was coming too quickly and my heart was shedding a little more of me with every beat. How can I choose one of these people I've grown to love? But I couldn't not choose, could I?

No, I couldn't live without Haley, my Haley. I'd have to make a decision, I'd have to save her life. I had assured her that I would stand by her through thick and thin, and it was a promise I had every intention of keeping.

"One."

He spun Haley around, so she was facing him, and he pulled back his arm to plunge the knife.

"Henry," I sobbed his name. "I choose Henry," my words blurted out of my mouth before I even had time to process.

"Very well," James said walking over to where Henry sat. He had lost a lot of blood and couldn't put up much of a fight.

"I'm so sorry Henry," I sobbed.

I looked him in the eye and for the first time, they glimmered with a mixture of fear and betrayal but he wasn't looking at me "Please, d-don't." Henry pleaded and those were the last words he'd ever speak.

James plunged the knife into Henry's back and Henry let out a gurgling scream. With a desperate cry, I attempted to rush forward, but Fifteen had already taken hold of me. James withdrew his knife and stepped away with a sadistic smile on his face. Only then did Fifteen let me go.

I sprinted to Henry, rested his head in my lap, and cried into his hair. "I'm sorry, I'm so sorry" The rest of the world no longer existed, it was just me and the man I killed. At that moment, nothing and no one else mattered, it could have been minutes or even hours later when Jason yanked me away from Henry. I screamed, cried, and fought, but it was no use, I had to leave him.

"What's the big deal?" James smirked. "All I did was stab him in the back, how's that any different from what you did?"

I was sobbing too hard to speak.

"Leave her alone," Jason glared. "Don't think that I won't kill you. Sure, they might kill me after but it would still be worth it."

Ashley grabbed his arm, keeping him from doing something stupid.

"I didn't think you'd be the one coming to her defense," James laughed. "So she's got both of you wrapped around her little finger? Competing for her affection? That's not gonna end well."

"Are we done here?" Ashley glared.

"Yeah, we're done, put your blindfolds on." James sighed. "I look forward to next time."

I don't even remember getting back to my room, but Jason carried me to my bed and put water on the nightstand.

"If you need anything, I'm here okay?" He said, "I've never really been good at comforting people, I never know the right thing to say. But if you need to scream and break something, or if you need to rant, I'm your guy. I've always been good at rage, maybe a little too good, the other emotions not so much. But that's beside the point, I'm a good listener, so whatever you need, I'll be here. And I'm apparently a good talker too because I keep rambling... sorry".

I lay sobbing on my bed, unable to respond, unable to move, unable to breathe. It was too overwhelming; I felt my life slipping away with each passing second. It should've been me. Why wasn't it me?

GAMES OF RUIN

"I'll come and check on you in a little while," Jason squeezed my arm before leaving the room.

I was in that state for what felt like a lifetime, wrapping my arms around my knees to try and make the pain go away. I sobbed until there were no tears left to fall. I was left in a state of paralysis, no longer here nor there, there was a film that separated me and the world. Jason and Ashley shared the responsibility of taking care of me even though it was my fault that Henry was dead.

The next day, Haley stayed with me. She curled up beside me, raking her hands through my hair, and she cried, the tears she hadn't cried yesterday. The only sound in the room was her sobs, and it somehow made it easier, knowing I wasn't the only one falling apart.

We stayed like that all day and my self-hatred grew with every waking hour. How could I have been so stupid? So thoughtless? I was the one to blame for Henry's death and that guilt would stay with me forever. I might not have been the one wielding the knife, but I killed him all the same.

Chapter Thirty

I spoke for the first time in a long time, and it made Haley flinch behind me.

"I'm sorry."

"Hey, look at me, you didn't do anything wrong," Haley said.

"I killed him, Haley," I whispered.

"You can't blame yourself. Maybe you should've taken the pill, but you couldn't have known that this was going to happen. James is the one responsible, not you."

"I don't think I can do this," I said refusing to look her in the eye.

"Don't talk like that, I need you. If you can't pull it together for yourself, then do it for me, do it for all of us."

"But I don't know if I can. I can't keep watching the people I love die, I won't."

"You have to, it isn't easy for any of us, but we have to keep fighting," she cried.

"Henry," I sobbed.

"I know," Haley said, "It's okay, I know."

"If life is supposed to be a blessing, then why does it feel like such a curse?" I asked.

"I don't know," she admitted with a sad smile.

"It's like my mind can never agree with my soul and it leaves my whole body dismembered with chaos," I said.

"What do you mean?" She asked.

"My soul begs to be free, to let go, to leave this God-forsaken planet. And my mind, well my mind is on constant overdrive, trying to simply survive. It's an exhausting and never-ending cycle." I said, "And if I'm being honest, my soul's winning."

"Your life is important Amanda, you might not be able to see it but I can. You're going to do incredible things with your life and I know it's hard right now. You loved Henry, we all did but he would want you to keep fighting and I know it's selfish but I need you." She whispered, "promise me you won't give up."

"I don't make promises I can't keep," I cried.

"Amanda, promise me," her voice was louder now. "I'm not asking you to fight for yourself, I'm asking you to fight for me and the rest of the group, don't let us down."

"I promise," I whispered.

She pulled me out of bed. "Now go get in the shower and then if you feel up to it, come join the group because everyone's worried about you."

"Shower?" I asked confused and for the first time, I looked at my body covered in his blood. I exited the room, desperate to get away as quickly as possible.

"Hey, you alright?" Ashley asked as I raced past them, I didn't even bother to answer. Instead, I closed the bathroom door, turned on the hot water, and allowed the water to rinse away my guilt.

GAMES OF RUIN

I looked down at the shower pan to see the pink water flowing down the drain. It was the last part of Henry I'd ever see, and I was both grateful and sad to see it go.

I continued watching it for a long time, but I didn't allow any tears to fall. The time for grief was over, and my eyes would have to bear the burden of the weight of unshed tears.

I got out of the shower when the water ran clear and looked at myself in the mirror. The incision from the scalpel made my face look as broken as I felt. But there was something different about myself now, something I hadn't seen the last time I looked in the mirror. My hazel eyes were aflame with the need for justice, or, more realistically, the longing for revenge.

I walked out of the bathroom a new person, this one fueled with brokenness and despair, but it was no longer my weakness, it was what made me strong. It was what made me a survivor.

I walked into the living room and sat beside Fifteen who immediately got up and retreated to his room.

"That was weird right?" I asked the group.

"Yeah, maybe he's not feeling too well," Ashley said.

"Or maybe he blames me for Henry's death," I said with my eyes at my feet, "I would understand, I blame myself too."

"Nobody blames you, it was the only decision. Henry was the one that was hurt he might've not made it," Ashley's words rushed out of her.

"Yeah... Well, I made that maybe a reality," My eyes raised from my feet to my hands.

"You can look at us," Jason said. "This wasn't your fault."

"I don't want to," I said still withholding eye contact.

"Why?" Ashley asked.

"Because," I said.

"Because why?" Haley joined the conversation.

"Because I don't want to see the pity in your eyes," I said, then continued when they didn't respond. "All I am to you is broken, right? I'm just a tragedy."

"You know what, yeah. You are a freaking tragedy, Amanda." Jason said, and his words felt like a bullet to the chest. "At this point, we all are. But that doesn't make you weak or incompetent, and you are so much more than just broken." Jason began to shout, "So look at us and let us love you. Not despite your brokenness but because of it, because even the little pieces of you are beautiful."

I looked up, and my eyes finally met theirs. I breathed in the tense air and what met me was more beautiful than I could have ever anticipated. Their eyes held sadness and fear, but there was also so much more. There was a softness that took me by surprise, a love I'd never felt. Is this what it feels like to be a part of a family?

"See, we're all the same Amanda, were broken fragments of the people we used to be. Losing Tristan hurt but when we lost Henry, it felt like a piece of me died and in a way, it did because we're all in this together," Ashley said.

"She's right," Haley said looking at me "I was wrong before, I told you that me and you stick together no matter what, but it's not like that anymore. Now it's all of us that have to stick together, we have to take care of each other because we're all we have."

"Thanks, guys," I said and the words came from a place of true appreciation. "I wouldn't make it without you."

"Ditto," Jason said with a sad smile, "we need you as much as you need us. Like it or not, you're stuck with us."

GAMES OF RUIN

For the next few hours, we all stayed together watching movies and talking. We all silently grieved the loss of Henry, but we weren't alone, and that made all the difference. Fifteen stayed in his room and refused to look at me on the rare occasion that he came out to use the bathroom or get a drink of water.

I assumed he wanted to take a moment to himself to process his grief. However, the others in the group claimed he was doing alright before I showed up.

I grappled with the idea that he blamed me for Henry's death and even though I tried to push the thoughts away, I was aware deep down that I was guilty. I avoided him as much as he avoided me because I couldn't bear to see the accusation in his eyes. I couldn't handle the thought of him seeing me the way I see myself.

Chapter Thirty-One

The guilt of Henry's death was weighing heavy on my soul, making it impossible to breathe. And why should I get to breathe when he never will again? I know I deserve all the pain and agony that my heart possesses, but that doesn't make this any easier.

I looked over to Haley, "I need a distraction."

"Let's go to my room," She immediately stood and at that moment, I was so grateful for her existence.

"Umm, let me think..." She paused, "What about the photos?"

"What about them?" I asked confused.

"Do you wanna talk about the girl in yours?"

"She's my sister kinda... I guess."

"Well that cleared things up," she chuckled without humor.

"We're biological sisters." I laughed an empty laugh, "But she has a new family now."

"That sounds juicy, you've been holding out on me," she tucked a strand of hair behind her ear, "explain."

I rolled my eyes but secretly I was grateful for the distraction.

"We were inseparable as kids, she was my best friend. But when my Mom and Dad got divorced, I stayed with my Mom, and she stayed with my dad."

"So you guys just drifted apart?"

"No, we were still close until my Dad remarried. He married a woman with two daughters about our age. It's pretty simple really, she got new sisters, and I was replaced."

Her eyes widened. "They just dropped you?"

"Pretty much, I tried to get in contact with them, and they just didn't want anything to do with me. I saw her at my Mom's funeral, but she didn't even acknowledge my existence."

"Shut up," she said.

"I'm serious, they tried to put me in foster care, but I just lived in my car. My foster parents never even noticed I was gone."

"I'm so sorry, that's awful," she said.

"No, I mean, it's okay. She's my sister, even if I'm not hers. I'll always love her," I said. "But enough about me, what about you? Who's the handsome guy?" I picked up the photo from her nightstand to get a closer look.

She laughed, "Just a friends-with-benefits situation we've had for years. I love him, but I'm not in love with him, that's all there really is to know."

"I share my life story and that's all I get?" I laughed, "You suck."

"The distraction worked didn't it?" She flashed me a smile and dramatically flipped her hair before leaving the room.

Eventually, when everyone had gone to sleep, I mustered up the courage to visit Fifteen's room and have the discussion I had been dreading all day. The hour had come to face the guilt, the shame, and the disappointment in his eyes.

I lingered by his door, my fists unwilling to knock. I didn't come prepared with any defenses, because I knew that I was in the wrong, but now I found myself wondering if I should have. All I did know was that I was responsible for Henry's death and that I wouldn't dispute that fact.

All I could do was apologize for killing Henry and hope he'd find it in his heart to forgive me. If he couldn't, I wouldn't hold it against him; I will never forgive myself either. But I could hope.

After what felt like a lifetime, I lifted my hand and knocked on his door before I had the chance to talk myself out of it.

"Come in," he said and after exhaling my pent-up anxiety, I opened the door and crossed the threshold.

"Hi, how are you holding up?" I asked.

"Fine," he was still refusing to look me in the eye.

"You don't seem fine, do you wanna talk about it?" I scanned his face for any remnants of positive emotion, all I found was rage.

"Nope," he said, and I had half a mind to retreat to my room, but I couldn't, not yet.

"Fifteen, look I know you cared about Henry, we all did, and I feel so guilty for choosing him. I'm so, so truly sorry that I got him killed and if I could go back and take that pill, nothing in this world could stop me. But I can't go back, and I couldn't let Haley die. I know it was selfish, but she's my best friend."

The silence hung in the air so I continued. "Anyway, what I'm trying to say is that I'm sorry, and I know that words aren't going to bring him back, but I'm not sure what else I can do." I remained there for what seemed like an infinite amount of time. I began to wonder if he was going to reply at all.

"Are you done?" Fifteen asked and I was astonished by his coldness.

"Yeah, that's all I needed to say," I spoke softly, willing this conversation to be over. I turned around to leave his room when I heard him speak.

"You know me, Amanda, do you really think that's what I'm mad about?"

"I don't know what to think," I admitted.

"Of course, you blame yourself for Henry's death, you blame yourself for everything." He paused, "James killed Henry, not you, and it's ridiculous that you'd think I was mad at you for something you had no control over." He ran his hand through his hair and stood up.

"Th-then what? I don't understand." I asked, completely taken off guard. He finally looked me in the eye and I swear his eyes were so blue I drowned.

"You know what Amanda? It sucks," he shouted, "that you see no value in your own life. It's bad enough to watch you struggle, to see the voice in your head win, to know how much blame you carry around. But what's so much worse is watching you sacrifice yourself time and time again." His eyes glazed over.

"Fifteen, stop," I whispered as tears formed in my eyes.

"No, let me finish. You think that you're worth less than everyone else, that you can't possibly be important. You think that just because you have flaws, you're some kind of mistake. But you just can't see what I see, you can't see how special you really are."

"You don't know what you're talking about," I pleaded with my eyes.

"Stop interrupting me, Amanda. "He growled, and I had no choice but to comply.

GAMES OF RUIN

"I'm not mad that you chose Henry, I'm mad that you were your first choice. Without hesitation, you chose to get yourself killed. You did the same thing with Tristan, you keep volunteering to die without thinking about what it would do to me."

"And what's that?" I asked, looking up at him.

"Isn't it obvious?" He asked, "I would be destroyed Amanda, I would fight through heaven and hell just to be by your side. Losing you is not an option. I won't sit around and watch you get yourself killed." His voice was softer now, and he walked over to where I was standing.

"Why not?" I asked because I needed to hear him say it.

He leaned his hand against the wall, pinning my body in place, and whispered, "Because despite all odds, I have fallen madly and deeply in love with you, and it absolutely terrifies me."

"Say it again," I whispered with pleading eyes.

"I love you, Amanda," he murmured, "and that's a scary enough thing in the real world. But here, it's a recipe for disaster. Every day poses a new threat, so I tried my hardest," he sighed.

"You tried to what?" My mind was fuzzy, for some reason, nothing was making sense, he was standing too close to me.

"I tried to stop myself from falling for you because I can't protect you here. But the harder I tried to stop it, the harder I fell. You mean everything to me so I can't just sit back and watch you sacrifice yourself time and time again. It hurts me too much, can't you see that?"

Before I had the chance to reply, he lifted my chin with his hand and he kissed me.

He kissed me and the darkness of the world around me vanished. He pulled away, and my lips ached with his absence. I pulled him in again, this time entangling my body with his. I needed to be closer to this man who I loved with all of me.

He somehow managed to push past my strongest internal defenses. What I felt wasn't exactly fireworks, instead, it was safe, it was right, and it was everything my body craved.

"Wait," it took all the strength I had to pull away. "You have a girlfriend," I whispered defeated.

"I do," he murmured, moving the hair out of my face.

"So..." My mind struggled to place words together, I had to think hard before forming a complete sentence. "So we can't."

"I think considering the circumstance and the fact that we might never make it out of here, I think it's okay. I can't exactly break up with her right now." His finger traced a line over my exposed shoulder as he spoke.

"So you would though?" I asked.

"What?"

"Break up with her?"

"Yes," he said with his eyes on my lips.

"Why?" I asked.

"Because she isn't you." He said it like it was the most obvious thing in the world. "Can I kiss you now?"

"Ye-" His lips crashed into mine, taking my breath away, stealing every ounce of rationality in my body. One of my hands was tangled in his hair while the other lay upon his chest, a reminder that his heart was pounding just as quickly as my own. I was so consumed by the moment that I didn't even hear the door open.

GAMES OF RUIN

"Is everything-" Jason said, then he saw us. "Never mind I heard yelling, so I came to... I guess everything's fine though, so I'm just gonna go."

"Yeah, I'm gonna go too," I said embarrassed. "Can we talk later?" I asked Fifteen.

"Yeah, see you tomorrow," he said after clearing his throat.

"Hey Jason, wait up," I rushed to his side.

"What's up?" He asked.

"I just wanted to say, thanks for checking in, I'm sorry that you walked in... I just don't want it to be awkward." I stammered.

"It's fine, it's not like you were naked" he laughed "We're good, and don't worry, I won't tell anyone"

"Thanks, Jason," I felt the heat emanating from my cheeks.

"But to be clear, anyone with eyes knows you two are in love," he laughed.

"I'm just glad that you found something good in such a terrible situation."

"You really are the best, you know that?"

"Of course I do," he grinned. "Now get some sleep, and I'll see you tomorrow."

I wrapped him in a hug then I pulled away and said "Goodnight."

"Night," he whispered, and we went to our rooms.

That night, a million thoughts raced through my mind. Everything with Fifteen felt right like it was meant to be but I wasn't foolish enough to believe in fairy tale endings. I was being held against my will in the scariest of places, I may not even make it out alive.

How stupid was I to believe this thing with Fifteen would end in any more than a disaster? Even though I knew better, I fell asleep with only one thought that consumed my mind. How lucky I am that God chose to make Fifteen exist at the same time as me.

Chapter Thirty-Two

The next day, Ashley woke me up early and pulled me into the bathroom where everyone was awaiting me. I hadn't even gotten time to wake up and confusion pricked at my brain.

"What's going on?" I asked still rubbing the sleep out of my eyes. "Did someone wake up Hen-" I stopped when I remembered he was dead, that I killed him.

Everyone looked at me with blank eyes.

"Sorry," I muttered as I tried to hold back tears, "I somehow forgot."

"It's okay," Haley whispered into my hair after pulling me in for a hug.

"We're breaking out," Ashley said so quietly, I could barely hear her over the running faucet.

"What do you mean? We can't." Haley straightened up.

"Woah, let's just wait and think this through," Fifteen's eyes widened.

"What about the photos?" I asked sleepily.

"Yeah, they could hurt the people we care about," Fifteen agreed.

"I don't know about you but everyone in this room is a person I care about. Don't get me wrong, I love my big brother but we can't keep doing this. How long until we're all dead?" Ashley asked and her face was devoid of emotion.

Henry's death had changed her, I hadn't seen her shed a tear in the last few days, the same Ashley that sobbed 24/7. Her eyes for once weren't puffy and raw, the need for revenge took the place of sadness. She was cold and angry but most of all, she was strong.

"Me and Ashley have been working on a plan to get out of here," Jason said, "but we all have to be on board."

"I-I don't know," Haley said, "If we get caught they'll kill us."

"Yeah, but if I'm going to die anyway, I'd rather go down fighting," I said.

"So you're with us?" Ashley looked at me so intently, I felt her presence in my soul.

For a brief moment, I thought about my sister and how they threatened to hurt her if I didn't comply. I'd give my own life to save hers any day but could I put her well-being above Fifteen and Haley's? Above Jason and Ashley's? The immediate answer was no. They are my family as much as she is and there are four of them and only one of her.

"Yeah, I'm with you," I said scanning the room. "Let's get the hell out of here."

"Well I'm not letting you go without me," Fifteen said bumping my shoulder with his, sending a jolt of electricity through my body.

"I'm in too," Haley said, "So what's the plan?"

Me and Haley were kicked out of the bathroom and forced to sit in the living room with the promise that they would find time to fill us in on the plan later. For now, it was our job to show the cameras that there was nothing out of the ordinary, that it was just another day.

"It sucks that Ashley's not feeling good," Haley said after we sat down on the couch. "I wish there was something we could do."

"I know but she'll be okay, Fifteen and Jason are taking care of her," I said.

"I know but still."

I nodded, "What do you wanna do today?" I asked changing the subject.

"I'm not sure. We could play a game?" she asked and I shook my head. Nothing seemed fun since Henry died, everything felt mundane as if my life stopped when his did and in a way, it kind of did.

"Not really in the mood. A movie?" I asked.

"Sure."

I put on a movie I'd never watched before.

"Hey Amanda?"

"Yeah?" I asked.

"Do you think we'll ever get out of here?"

"Honestly... I don't know but we can hope right?"

"I guess. What do you think we're going to have to do for the next level?" She paused, "I can't keep doing this."

"I don't know, all we can do is pray to God that it isn't fatal," I said. "But we'll get through whatever it is, we've got each other."

"That's what I'm worried about," she said.

"Me too," I whispered and we watched the rest of the movie in silence. Surviving truly was the worst, all life's problems would be solved if I were dead, but of course, it's never that easy.

After a while, Ashley, Jason, and Fifteen came out of the bathroom and joined us on the couch.

"Are you okay, Ash?" I drowned my voice in sympathy.

"Yeah, I'm feeling a little better, still pretty nauseous though," she put a hand on her stomach.

"Just take it easy today," Haley said bringing her a cup of water. "Stay hydrated," she stared sternly at Ashley.

"Yes ma'am," Ashley said rolling her eyes but she drank the water anyway.

"What's the game plan for level three?" Jason asked knowing good and well we didn't plan on sticking around to find out.

"We don't really have one," Haley said.

"I think maybe let's wait for our clue, then we'll talk about it. I don't really wanna think about it yet," I shifted in my seat.

"Yeah me either," Fifteen said then he looked at me. "You wanna maybe go somewhere private?"

I instantly felt the heat rush to my face. I was angry he asked in front of everyone but even anger couldn't stop the excitement pumping through my veins. How pathetic.

"Oooh, it's getting real," Ashley teased.

"First comes love, then comes marriage then-" Haley chanted.

"Shut up," I laughed as my face turned red.

Jason winked at me but didn't say a word.

We walked into the bathroom and before Fifteen even closed the door all the way, I spoke.

GAMES OF RUIN

"What was that?" I glared, letting my eyes speak. "You can't just do that."

He turned on the faucet. "Last I checked, I was my own man I can do whatever I like," amusement danced in his voice.

He began to walk toward me, "Not when-" I stopped when his lips were mere inches from mine. My breath caught in my lungs.

"When what?" He teased and before I could answer, his lips came crashing into mine. When logic seeped into my mind, I abruptly pulled away.

"We're not doing this," I said remembering my anger.

"Why?" he whispered with his eyes still on my lips.

"Not until you tell me why you said that in front of everyone," I said crossing my arms.

"You're cute when you're angry," he said stepping close.

"Shut up," I rolled my eyes.

"It's part of the plan," he whispered, "I needed you in here to tell you how we're breaking out."

"Oh," I said, feeling stupid, "so tell me."

Chapter Thirty-Three

That evening, I found myself unable to sleep. With tomorrow's escape attempt looming, the plan was on a loop, consistently playing in my mind. It wasn't perfect, the people in charge went to great lengths to make sure we couldn't escape. I wasn't stupid enough to believe that it was going to be easy.

An infinite number of things could go wrong, and by tomorrow evening, everyone I love could be dead. If the punishment for not swallowing a pill was so harsh, I couldn't even begin to fathom the repercussions if they discovered us attempting to escape. That thought terrified me, but even still, we couldn't not try. We couldn't sit back and let our group disintegrate one by one.

That night, I prayed harder than I'd ever prayed before and hoped it was enough. The God above is merciful and I had faith he'd lead us to safety. Despite many hours of lying in bed, unable to sleep, I eventually rose to get a glass of water, only to find myself knocking on Fifteen's door instead.

"Hey," I said after he opened the door.

"Late-night booty call?" He laughed.

"Shut up," I leaned against his doorway, "I couldn't sleep."

"Yeah, me either." He said, his voice serious now. "You wanna stay in here with me tonight?"

"Is that okay?" I asked, trying not to sound too eager.

"Always," he climbed in bed and scooted over to make room for me. We stayed like that for a long time until I finally spoke.

"Fifteen, I'm scared," I whispered.

"I know, I am too," his voice sounded distant like he was millions of miles away. I felt safe in his arms; that was the last thing I remembered before drifting off to sleep.

When it was time to get up and eat breakfast, I had only slept for about an hour. Nevertheless, I woke Fifteen up but I was too nervous to appreciate his sleepy smile. His smile dissipated after a few moments as his mind remembered what today was.

"It's time for breakfast," my voice was soft.

"Five more minutes," he propped his head up.

Was he serious? All our lives were at stake and he wanted to go back to bed? I saw his eyes flick to the camera, just slightly, enough for me to notice. Then all of a sudden I understood. He was trying to show the cameras that today was a normal day. And what would a new couple do on a normal day? They'd take a moment to be together before heading out to be with the group.

"Fine, but only a couple of minutes," I relented, trying to sound as normal as possible, "I want to check on Haley."

His finger traced my jawline in response. One mere touch made my stomach twirl. He turned my face to kiss him but I turned away.

"I have morning breath," I chuckled. "Maybe after I've brushed my teeth."

"I'm going to hold you to that," he whispered in my hair.

"It's been a couple of minutes," I sighed, "time to eat, I'm starving".

He groaned in protest as he slowly got out of bed. "But Haley doesn't need you as much as I do."

I playfully glared at him, "So we're already having the best friend vs. boyfriend obstacle? I thought that we still had a few months."

He rolled his eyes, " I'd never dream of fighting Haley for your affection."

"Good," I flipped my hair, "because that's a fight you'd always lose."

"Liar," he chuckled as he opened the door and we went to join the others. They had already gathered at the table. We made small talk, so the cameras didn't detect anything amiss, but the tension in the air was unmaskable. We were all acting, and we had no choice but to put on a good show. It was life and death.

After our meal, we all gathered in the living room to watch a movie. But none of us were actually watching it, we were all in the depths of our thoughts.

"They should be giving us the meds today," Ashley said.

"What do you think they're gonna do to us?" Haley asked.

"I don't know, but I think we'll be okay," Jason plopped his face into his hands.

"I hope so," Haley began to tear up.

"It'll be alright," I whispered giving Haley a tight hug "I love you, Haley," I said, my own eyes starting to swell.

"I love you too," she said pulling away. If everything was going to work out fine, then why did this feel so much like a goodbye? My paranoia began to cloud my mind and suddenly, I was petrified.

As if on cue, we heard the all-familiar sound of the door buzzing unlocked and a nurse walked in with five cups of pills. All of us got together and collected the cups, apart from Fifteen who began to shout.

"Who do you think you are?" He asked stepping towards her. "How can you do this to us and still live with yourself?"

The distraction was working, she was looking at Fifteen. We all pretended to take our pills and stayed out of sight of the cameras.

"Calm down dude," Jason said, "just take the pills, you know what happens if you don't." There was a threatening quality to his voice.

"But Jason, they can't make us-" Fifteen eyes flicked between the nurse and Jason.

"Now, Matthew," Jason didn't back down.

"Whatever," Fifteen said, taking the pills from the nurse and swallowing them without water. He glared at her with a hate buried deep in his soul.

The nurse examined our mouths to confirm we had swallowed the pills. Then to our surprise, she spoke.

"Thanks for complying, I hate to see you suffer but just know it's for a good cause. So many people will be forever indebted to you." Following that, she exited the room.

"What the hell was she talking about?" Jason asked.

"I have no idea," I said as we all stared dumbfounded at the door.

"A good cause?" Ashley stammered, "Is she serious?"

"I don't know," I said.

GAMES OF RUIN

Why was everyone looking to me for answers?

Fifteen excused himself to go to the bathroom, we didn't even acknowledge his absence, we were all too distracted.

"Let's just sit down," Jason said. "She's obviously lost it."

We sat there in silence for what felt like an eternity. Fifteen joined us again, they would know he threw up his pill but at this point, it hardly mattered. If the plan worked out, we wouldn't be here for his punishment anyway.

"Does anyone feel tired?" I asked, it was the cue phrase.

"Yeah, a little," Jason whispered.

Seconds later, we all lolled our heads and relaxed our muscles.

It was go time.

We stayed like that for so long, that I had begun to question if anyone was actually going to come.

Internally I began to panic, *they knew. Somehow they knew. No, that's crazy they couldn't know*, my mind was in a fierce argument with itself. My brain was flooded with Anxiety and Paranoia, the ultimate duo.

I had to control myself from shuddering when the noise of the door being opened eventually reached my ears. I coerced my eyelids to stay closed until I heard a commotion. By the time my eyes shot open, Fifteen had already knocked out a nurse and Jason was going after the second.

"Normally, I'd never hurt a girl but extraordinary circumstances and all that," Fifteen said.

Jason knocked out the other and her body slumped to the ground. "What he said."

Chapter Thirty-Four

Fifteen grabbed my hand and without a second to spare, we began running as fast as our feet would take us.

"Fifteen?" I managed between breaths.

"Yeah?" He asked.

"For what it's worth, I love you too."

"It's worth more than you know, but we're going to make it." He said urging me faster.

I planted step after rugged step, following the route we had all come up with together, praying we were going in the right direction. It felt right like we were running to freedom, but we were previously blindfolded, and we may have misremembered a turn. That thought haunted my very soul. This place was bigger than I ever could have imagined, not that I had time to look at the scenery.

I ran by what felt like hundreds of rooms. My lungs were screaming for air, and we hadn't even gotten halfway. Like the room we stayed in, everything was white. As soon as I get out of here, I'm never looking at that color again, I'll wear black to my wedding.

My breaths became more rapid, trying to keep up with my pounding heart. I found myself wishing that I had exercised with all my time in captivity. If it wasn't for the adrenaline, my body would have crashed a long time ago. But we were nearing the end, and we hadn't seen anyone yet, I thanked God for that fact.

"I don't know if I can keep going," Haley huffed.

"We have to Hales, we're almost free," I begged her to keep going.

"I need a minute," Jason said, and we came to a crashing halt. The cut on his foot had reopened, and his face showed his pain.

"Just a second man," Fifteen said. "We have to keep going, lean on me if you need to."

Fifteen helped Jason along and our pace slowed a little. As my heartbeat calmed, my thoughts intensified. I searched every inch of the hallway and I knew deep down that we were running out of time.

"Just leave me," Jason said, "I'll catch up."

"Nobody's leaving anyone," I said. "We'll make it," I didn't let my doubtfulness show in my voice.

We were so close, I could see trees ahead. Everything in my body lurched forward, I let hope lead me on. I heard the sound of footsteps behind me and I became physically sick with fear. I turned my head to see a whole army of people, heading straight for us.

"We have a problem," I said as tears began to swell up in my eyes, I shoved them down.

"We have to go, *NOW!*" Fifteen screamed after seeing them.

We all ran faster with adrenaline guiding our feet. There was only one door left, and we had to get there before they locked it. I sprinted ahead, using all the energy my body possessed. My muscles were crying out in pain, and my lungs were begging for more air. I ignored them all, pushing my body past its limit until I reached the door.

"Please," I whispered as I shoved with all my might. It broke open, unlocked, and I cried tears of relief. I looked back to Fifteen and Jason, and the relief quickly dissipated. They were gaining on them and fast.

As I saw the horror unfold, I felt my face go pale.

"You have to hurry," I screamed, "They're right behind you." My whole body crumbled at the scene before me, I watched as they grabbed hold of Jason and Fifteen tried to fight them off.

"Go," Jason said when he was no longer able to fight them off. There were too many of them and they just kept coming. "You have to go get help," he pleaded. Then louder this time when Fifteen didn't listen, "If you want to help me, you have to go."

"We'll come back for you, stay alive," Fifteen hesitated before breaking out from the crowd.

My whole body ran towards the danger, I couldn't abandon Jason, he was my family.

"Amanda don't, all we can do for him now is go get help," Fifteen said, dragging me along.

"We can't leave him," I begged.

"We have no choice," his eyes were sad as he looked at Jason one last time.

I didn't want to believe it but deep down I knew he was right. So I did the only thing I could do. I ran with everything I had, towards the swaying trees and prayed that my feet would take me fast enough.

I heard Jason yell, but I didn't slow down, there was nothing I could do for him now.

"I love you, Ashley," Was the last thing I heard him say before they dragged him away.

I looked at Ashley, her demeanor was cold and angry. There was not a single tear in her eyes, she was determined and set in her ways. When did our Ashley get so strong?

Henry's death had broken something inside of her and I worried she'd never recover. Then again, I don't think any of us had a shot of getting our old selves back. This was our reality now and all we could do was fight.

"We made it," Haley said beside us.

"Not until we've lost them, not until we've gotten help," I huffed between breaths.

"We'll make it." Fifteen said, "We have to, for Jason."

That one fact was the only thing keeping our bodies from collapsing. The only thing allowing our feet to take step after step. It was our inspiration to keep moving forward when everything told us to quit. Our friend needed our help.

We ran for what felt like an eternity. It was the four of us against the world. I let hope engulf me entirely, this was our moment. We weren't safe yet but I could almost taste the freedom.

I stopped suddenly, and the others followed suit looking at me confused, waiting for direction.

"We lost them," Haley frantically looked around.

I gulped, the whole world spun around me and bile threatened to come up. This was too easy.

"No," I said, "they stopped chasing us."

"What? Why would they-" Ashley's eyebrows pulled together and I watched as understanding covered her face. I saw the exact moment that her broken soul shattered even more.

"No, no, no," Haley whispered with a shaking voice.

I looked at Fifteen, only to see an emptiness that hadn't been there before. His eyes were devoid of any emotion, as though his soul was no longer in his body.

I stared at the trees, unable to move, unable to speak, unable to breathe. My whole body iced over, my heart slowed to an ungodly rhythm and the only thing I was even sure of anymore was the fear that drenched my entire body.

The light in the sky suddenly dimmed, confirming my worst nightmare.

None of this is real.

"Welcome to the hunt," the intercom sang in a cheerful voice.

That was the moment that killed my soul.

Coming Soon

Book Two of this trilogy will be coming soon! Games of Heartache will begin where Games of Ruin ends. It will almost read like a really big book! If you're interested in finding out what will happen to Amanda West and her friends. Or want to find out who her captors are and why they're doing this, stay tuned for updates.

Follow me on Tiktok for real-life updates and news! tiktok.com/@K.J.Rivers

Made in the USA
Monee, IL
24 January 2024